T0104480

No
SENSE *of*
HUMOR

Quest For The Title: Part Two

Nick Morgan

Order this book online at www.trafford.com
or email orders@trafford.com

Most Trafford titles are also available at major online book retailers.

© Copyright 2014 Nick Morgan.
All rights reserved. No part of this publication may be reproduced,
stored in a retrieval system, or transmitted, in any form or by
any means, electronic, mechanical, photocopying, recording, or
otherwise, without the written prior permission of the author.

Printed in the United States of America.

ISBN: 978-1-4907-3166-7 (sc)
ISBN: 978-1-4907-3165-0 (e)

Because of the dynamic nature of the Internet, any web addresses or
links contained in this book may have changed since publication and
may no longer be valid. The views expressed in this work are solely those
of the author and do not necessarily reflect the views of the publisher,
and the publisher hereby disclaims any responsibility for them.

Any people depicted in stock imagery provided by Thinkstock are models,
and such images are being used for illustrative purposes only.
Certain stock imagery © Thinkstock.

Trafford rev. 03/20/2014

 www.trafford.com

North America & international
toll-free: 1 888 232 4444 (USA & Canada)
fax: 812 355 4082

CONTENTS

PREFACE

Now that you have had a glimpse of what the adult characters look like, let us take a look at what Beth created for the ladies' second and final title-quest. Most of you will probably think that this title-quest will be similar to the title-quests in the past. I was amazed at what Beth created for this story-line. Not only are the men excluded from this title-quest, but the rules for the title-quest have changed. It certainly puts a twist on how one would vote for the best narrated story.

Once again, let's add the mixture of revised stories, pranks and the competitive nature of our pet characters. In this book you will get a chance to see the humor in how cats and dogs find ways to out-do the other, whether it would come from a contest or from a devious plan. Either way, it sure would be entertaining to find out which organization wins in the end. I wish I could say that these stories will set the stage for a preview of coming attractions. It will only be found in the famous unanswered questions. Despite the rivalry between the adult characters and the rivalry between the pets that might show you that they have a sense of humor, my version of the story-line will guarantee you I don't have a sense of humor, for the 8th time.

LIST OF CHARACTERS

Author: Pet owner to Sophie. Second Oldest in group. Looks at ads in newspapers for famous half-time quotes. Gave up drinking on poker nights. Has 16 pairs of reading glasses in junk draw. Now plays state lottery twice a week in the hopes that he wins money to move to Florida. Still wears **N. S. O. H.** baseball cap on dates. Was convinced by Rick to post an on-line dating profile. Wants to write 32 more sequels before retiring. Addicted to coffee. Favorite Music: Country.

Marty: Author's weekly poker buddy. Has father who owns novelty chain. Youngest in group. Former pet owner to Ralph. Dreads owing Author a favor. Convinced men to boycott ladies' title-quest. Decided to grow a beard. Has Cindy convinced it makes him look sexier. Wants to write Author's famous half-time quote. Still recovering from sprained ankle. Invested in Eli and Walter's publishing business without consulting Cindy. Employment Status: Teacher at local University.

Rick: Wants to date one of the models from the beauty contest. Brings jelly beans to poker nights. Now works as an editor for a local newspaper. Dreams of becoming a novelist. Former pet owner to Lulu. Formerly married to Jill. In competition with Author to collect restraining orders. Always well dressed. Favorite Food: Peanut Butter & Jelly Sandwiches. Employment Status: Used Car Salesman. Favor Music: Jazz.

Harry: One of Author's poker buddies. Former computer repairman, now retired. Oldest in group of degenerates. Bought another Parrot for Harriett. Takes on-line course in humor. Took up paint-by- numbers as new hobby. Brings donuts to poker nights. Takes care of Sophie when Author is out of town on business. Favorite Music: None.

Harry Sr.: Veteran. Married to Eve. Harry's father. Employment Status: Retired. Always wears stretchy pants. Favorite Hobby: Eating Eve's lasagna. Newest addition to Men's poker night. Still convinced Author is a nut job. Favorite Music: Jazz.

Cindy: Beloved wife to Marty. Extremely jealous of Beth. Participant in new ladies title-quest. Lead female character. Addicted to Fudge-Ripple ice cream. Wants to write book about men. Sells home-made products on-line. Wants to write book about men. Favorite Music: Pop.

Cynthia: Dating Status: Single. Close friend to Cindy. Participant in new ladies title-quest. Returned for Cindy's famous margaritas. Can handle talking pets after several drinks. Wants to have Author return use of Strip-O-Grams. Favorite Snack: Carrots. Favorite Music: Rock & Roll.

Harriett: Married to Harry. Participant in new ladies title-quest. Proud owner of Daisy Mae. Parent to Cassandra. Former title-holder. Does home sewing projects. No longer addicted to Strip-O-Grams. Employment Status: Housewife. Favorite Music: Country. Favorite Food: Watermelon.

Bertha: Former resident of the Soviet Union. Nurse Practitioner. Works at local Children's Hospital. Former Olympian. Participant in new ladies title-quest. Still wears latex gloves. Took second place in country dance contest. Favorite Music: Classical. Favorite Food: Eve's lasagna.

Brenda: Publishing consultant. Now works free-lance for two publishing companies. Participant in new ladies title-quest. Renaldo's former Fiancé. Favorite Music: Rock & Roll.

Anna: Former Russian Model. Speaks four languages. Employment Status: Banker. Leader of the Canine Mafia. Participant in new ladies title-quest. New Hobby: Making wood cabinets. Dating Status: Single. Favorite Music: Country. Favorite Snack: Pretzels.

Beth: Writing Assistant. Formerly from Soviet Union. Pet owner to Nani. Got her first tattoo after the second story went to print. Will keep her tattoo secret until book nine. Favorite Food: Eve's lasagna. Favorite Music: Rock & Roll.

Eve: Beloved wife of Harry Sr. Excellent cook. Constantly tries to teach her husband how to play the piano. Favorite Music: Opera. Wants Author to make improvements on His and Hers remote controls.

Annie: Co-leader of the Cat Mafia. Hates men and all of the pet characters. Loves stealing money from canines. Dating Status: Single. Best friend to Amy. Former neighbor to Author. Former Victoria's Secret model. Novelty expert, trained by Amy. Favorite Food: Spaghetti. Favorite Signature move: Places black licorice at every crime scene.

Ralph: Canine. Dalmatian. Male. Married to Mary Ann. Sophie's former boyfriend. Publisher to "No sense of Humor" books. Best friend and partner to Tom. Started drive-thru at novelty store. Has a litter of eight. Father to Ruby; Queen of Prankster School for Pets. Marty's former pet. Former Bus Boy, DEA Agent, Waiter. Favorite Food: Chinese.

Tom: Feline. Male. Siamese. Best friend to Ralph. Former leader of the Cat Mafia. Married to Penny. Loves taking bubble baths. Has sister that works in FBI. Favorite Hobby: Making canine statues. Ralph's business partner.

Co-Owner of Paws R Us. Favorite Food: Spinach. Favorite Movie: Cats & Dogs.

Sophie: Canine. Golden Retriever. Female. Has photo on covers of books 1, 3, and 4. Local celebrity. Still wants to win the lottery. Beloved pet of Author. Updates Facebook account daily. Thinks aroma therapy is used to disguise Ralph's farts. Wants to win Lottery. Favorite Pet Character: Jack.

Eli: Feline. Male. Started new Cat publishing company with Walter. Former henchman of the Cat Mafia, went straight. Takes baths only with rubber Ducks, courtesy of Bruce. Favorite Food: Chicken. Favorite Music: None

Walter: Feline. Male. Started new Cat publishing company with Eli. Former henchman of the Cat Mafia, went straight. Wants to become a chef. Takes cooking lessons from Sophie. Favorite Food: Bacon & Eggs. Favorite Music: Classical.

Ben: Raccoon. Male. Former Director of lake camp site. Returned for one story. Wants to marry a British Rock-Star. Records canine pranks for Author. Favorite Food: Anything. Favorite Music: Jazz

Zeke: Alien. Green. Married. Has four of everything. New best friend to Mr. High Pockets. Has 227 children. Wants to move to planet Earth with family. Planet of Origin:

Zorba. Favorite TV Game Show: Spin the Zorba. Favorite Food: Beans & Wieners.

Mr. High Pockets: Canine. Male. Jack Russell Terrier. Nicknamed the "Yapper". Currently the Mayor of Dogville. Former dispatcher to Canine Mafia. Former employee of Camp Paws.

BEGINNING THE QUEST

What were the men thinking when they allowed themselves to give in to another title-quest for the ladies? Was it because the men decided to be nice for a change? Or was it because the men had an ulterior motive? Actually, it was the men themselves and their hormones that got the better of them. This was something that I could not understand. How did the men allow it to happen in the first place? Here is what I am stumped on. Marty and Harry Sr. have it made. They have wives that adore them and spoil them rotten. One would think that these men have it too good, at least according to Rick. However, my faithful companions acted as if they had never seen an attractive woman before. If you remember correctly, they acted the same way when Beth was first introduced. Even the ladies dressed elegantly for their men on the night of the beauty contest. It was the ladies subtle hint to the men for them to look and not touch. Next time the men should not make it so obvious to the ladies of their secret desires. Wars have started by far less.

During our last poker night, the men were constantly griping about their lack of awareness regarding the contest. Marty said *"How could we be so gullible?"* Rick was okay with the event since he was the only single male that hoped the event would improve his social life. Harry Sr. only wanted lasagna but enjoyed the fact that judging a beauty contest and being away from Eve for an evening was just as good as winning the Lottery. To him, chances like that only come once in a lifetime. After Rick dealt the first round of cards, Marty said to me *"How can you let that happen to us?"* I gave Marty a look so that he knew I was not the guilty party. When he shook his head, I said *"Me?"* and then added *"How the heck was it my fault? It was your hormones that went wacko that night."* I could then tell that from the look on Harry's face that he was having fun at Marty's expense. Even though the men got themselves into trouble, I had to figure out a way to save their dignity. If I didn't, I would never hear the end of it. So, in being the good Author that I am, I told the men that I will see to it that the ladies don't have total control of their upcoming title-quest.

The following Saturday morning I called Beth to have the ladies meet me at the coffee shop so that we could go over the so-called "Rules of Engagement" for the title-quest. Before the ladies arrived, I decided to come up with a unique system on how the contest will be judged. With any luck, the ladies will not try to convince me to give in to their demands. I think it's safe to assume that the ladies do know how to get their way. This was one time I had to be strong since the rest of men were not up to the task. So, I put on my game face, placed the folders on the table and waited for the ladies to arrive.

Beth was the first to arrive at the coffee shop. She ordered her usual and as she approached the table, the rest of the ladies arrived with the same enthusiasm as Beth. It didn't take long for the ladies to get settled into their chairs and give me that popular look. Smiling, I thanked the ladies for arriving on such short notice. The folders that I had placed on the table were marked for each of the ladies to read. Inside were the complete instructions for the title-quest. For this title-quest, I told the ladies that they would get only one chance to narrate a story to a panel of Judges. The panel would consist of myself, Adam and another male Judge that would be announced on the day of the contest. Each story would be evaluated on its uniqueness. Pranks were allowed within the story-line. The stories have to be written by each lady with no outside help. Rules such as the use of the famous timer and the "Exclusionary Rule" would be enforced.

Cindy gave me a disgruntled look and said *"Does your highness want anything else?"* as she crossed her arms. I told the ladies there was more as I then handed them a list of what novelties could be used. I then said *"The men are not allowed to interfere. They can be used or hired to help you set up pranks but they cannot help you with the story."* As soon as I made that comment, all of the ladies looked at each other. I could sense their brains were working overtime when they smiled. Far be it for me to change their looks but out of respect for the men I said *"By the way, the men will be used as observers on the day of the contest."* Cynthia looked at me and said *"What do you mean observers?"* I told the contestants that the men would be used as observers only and that since they cannot interfere with the narration of the stories, they could however be used as a distraction. It seemed to me at that point that the ladies were more intrigued with the use of the distractions than they were with narrating the stories.

Once I refilled my coffee, I gave the ladies the rest of the details for the contest. I told the ladies that the contest will be held the following Saturday at high noon at our famous park. Cindy looked at the ladies and then said to me *"Why can't we have the contest at my house?"* I told Marty's wife that I felt the contest should be judged on neutral grounds so that no contestant had an advantage over the other. With hesitation, I gave the ladies their final instruction. I said *"By the way, no margaritas this time."* Harriett said *"At least he didn't take away our strip-o-grams."* I then said to Harriett *"Oh, that too."* Brenda shook her head as if she didn't agree with the rules. She asked me what would happen if the ladies did not abide by the rules. I told Brenda *"It's either the rules or the men get to have a title-quest of their own."* If Marty and the rest of men could have seen the looks on the ladies faces when I made that comment they would have been proud of me. As the ladies left with frowned looks, I wished the ladies luck.

The Solicitation Phase

Two Outs. Bottom of the ninth inning. The score is tied at six apiece. At least that's what I jokingly told the ladies before they started their quest for an accomplice. Cindy didn't waste any time in attempting to solicit her husband's help. She spent most of the day preparing a lavish meal and dressed so provocatively that there was no way Marty was going to turn her down. Cindy lit the candles in the dining room, turned on the stereo to listen to her favorite romantic song and sat in Marty's recliner. When Marty arrived home, he was only in the mood for a long, hot shower, a drink and a peaceful evening. According to him, he had a day at the office that was far from productive. He walked in the door and the first thing he said was *"Hi honey. Man I am glad to be home. What a day I had."* Marty froze in his tracks when he saw his beloved wife sitting in his recliner wearing his favorite tie. She said *"Hope you like the tie I picked out for you."* Before Marty could comment on his wife's appearance, Cindy rose from her seat and gave Marty a tender kiss, reminding him of how it used to be like when they first got married. Cindy grabbed Marty by the hand and sat him down on the sofa, poured him his favorite drink, loosened his tie and massaged his neck.

Marty at first was more than pleased to what greeted him when he arrived home but soon realized that Cindy was up to something. Far be it for Marty to ruin a good thing so he patiently went along with his wife's flirtatious ways. Cindy then whispered into her husband's ear *"After dinner, we can have dessert upstairs."* pointing to the bedroom. Marty could not resist a playful comment so he said *"Wow. All this and cheesecake too."* Even though Cindy wanted to clobber her husband for the comment he made, she refrained from using the "Marty" bat until she could get her way. During dinner, Cindy discussed the rules of the title-quest with her husband. She then rubbed her foot on Marty's leg and asked him *"Honey, will you help me?"* Marty smiled at his wife and said *"So, what's in it for me?"* Cindy gave her husband a very angry look and said *"What? This isn't good enough for you?"* while she pointed to the outfit that she was wearing. Marty's wife rose from her seat in disgust and headed to the bedroom not to be seen for the rest of the evening. I guess it was safe to assume that Cindy needed to find another patsy to help with her pranks.

Meanwhile, Harriett had the same intentions as Cindy but knew that trying a romantic version of solicitation would not work on Harry. Instead, she used a more common approach. During lunch, Harriett placed several magazines on the table. The magazines were Harry's favorite. After the rebuilding stage for the canines, Harry got more involved in wood-working projects at home. Previously, Harry had to stop work on a particular project because he needed new power tools. Harriett took it upon herself to order a new skill saw for her husband. To add to the enticement, she circled several brands of skill saws listed in the magazines so that her husband would have no problem picking out the one he liked the best. Harry knew his wife all too well. Besides, word had already spread to the men that the ladies were going to attempt to solicit their help. Harry said *"Dear, that is so thoughtful of you."* While Harriett was smiling thinking that her plan was working, Harry added *"Okay dear, what gives?"* Harriett at first tried to play that sweet, innocent role as just a loving and devoted wife. But when Harriett saw that her husband was not buying her story she said *"I want revenge on Mr. High Pockets."* Of course Harry knew why his wife wanted revenge in the worst way possible but told his wife *"But honey, he is our Yapper."* Harriett quickly replied *"So, what's your point?"* Harry could not give his wife a good reason. He finally said *"Okay, count me in."*

With two down and four to go, seems that Harriett's team now had the lead. One would think that it would be harder for the other ladies to solicit help since they were single. Let's see if being single has its advantages.

Cynthia had been out of the realm of pranks and story-telling for quite some time. A lot has changed since her departure so she knew that it was not going to be an easy task to solicit help. That day, Cynthia went over her list to see who she could find that would be the perfect patsy. Her smile indicated she found one person that would help her. Cynthia called Rick and asked him if she would have dinner with her that evening. Rick was not about to turn down a date with Cynthia. Cynthia picked a very romantic restaurant to set the stage for her plan. She figured that with Rick being single and having all of those dating profiles that Rick would certainly give in to her. For most of the evening, Cynthia's plan was working. Rick couldn't take his eyes off of Cynthia. I think that Rick was overjoyed with how Cynthia dressed than he was with the meal. Cynthia said to herself *"I have him right where I want him."* She then placed her hand on his and suggested that the two go for a romantic walk in the park.

The park as you know by now was our place in heaven, or, according to the rest of the female adult characters, a place that should have been converted into a parking lot after the last series of pranks had been played. At this time, Cynthia had not been told of what had happened in the park from previous stories. To her, it was just a way to put the icing on the cake. One final step in securing Rick's help. As the pair walked hand-in-hand along the path, Cynthia noticed the gazebo. She saw that the gazebo would be the perfect place to play her final card. As they strolled to the gazebo, Rick said to his date *"This is our famous gazebo."* Before Cynthia asked about the gazebo, she noticed that above her head nesting in a rafter was a beehive. Startled, she grabbed Rick by the hand and said *"Oh no, that's not good."* Rick smiled at Cynthia and said *"Don't worry. That one is fake. It was probably left over from one of Ralph's pranks."* To demonstrate to his date that the beehive was one of the novelties that contained candy, he positioned Cynthia beneath the beehive and said *"Just watch. Soon it will be raining candy."* Cynthia smiled in anticipation as she watched Rick strike the beehive. Instead of bees or candy, Cynthia was greeted with a treat that was not what she had hoped for. As she looked up when the beehive opened, she found herself completely covered in chocolate syrup.

Rick said "*I am so sorry. I thought the beehive contained candy.*" That comment was not the kind of apology Cynthia was looking for. The chocolate syrup that suddenly covered her provocative and sparkly dress now made her look like a chocolate sundae. Slowly Cynthia raised her head to give Rick that evil look. Yep, the same look Marty always gets from his wife whenever he gets in trouble. Frustrated was not the emotion I would describe what Cynthia was feeling at the time. Despite her efforts to find an object to throw at Rick in an attempt to relieve her frustrations, Cynthia stormed off into the night leaving Rick to ponder his prankster ways and fend for himself. Rick called me to pick him up. I arrived at the park and after Rick told me of what had happened to Cynthia I said to him jokingly "*Seems that with you dating has taken on a whole new meaning.*" On the way home, I could not resist another comment. I said "*At least you have Mindy's phone number.*"

For those of you who have not read the "First Ever No Sense of Humor Contest" in the last book, Mindy was portrayed as a single beauty contestant who undoubtedly did not possess the required beauty. Instead, she was known as a fart champion who had a major crush on Rick. Rest assure that if this woman would have demonstrated her championship status at the park, destroying the gazebo would have been a thought Cynthia liked. Even though Cindy and Cynthia did not have the luck they had hoped for in obtaining help for their pranks, there was one woman that had the capability to win anyone over to her side. Brenda certainly knew all of the characters very well. In fact, she knew the characters better than they did themselves. When Brenda went over her list, she knew there was one person who she could entice for the right price. It was Harry Sr. But first, she had to go through Eve. Eve was still a little sore from her husband's escapades in that beauty contest. Once Brenda explained to Eve of her intentions, Eve was more than happy to help. She told Brenda that if her plan got Harry Sr. out of the house and out of her hair for a day, it was worth it. Together, they cooked up a meal befitting a king in an attempt to convince Harry Sr. that his help was desperately needed.

Shortly before Harry Sr. woke from his afternoon nap, Brenda and Eve placed all of the cooked dishes on the table. They both knew that as soon as the aroma of freshly baked dishes maneuvered its way throughout the house Harry Sr. would soon follow. Sure enough, Harry Sr. walked into the kitchen clad only in shorts and said *"I smell food. Let's eat."* To his surprise, Harry Sr. saw a lavish spread on the table. Before Eve's husband could comment on the food, he went to the refrigerator and performed his daily after-nap ritual of drinking his favorite drink directly from the bottle. Eve whispered to Brenda *"Do you have to bring him back?"* after the ladies witnessed Harry Sr. wipe his mouth on his t-shirt. Harry Sr. finally noticed Brenda and said *"Hey cutie. What brings you to my castle?"*

She told the not-so-mannered Harry Sr. that she wanted to do something special for him after what he did for her at the beauty contest. Brenda then prepared a sampler plate of all of the delicious food she and Eve prepared and placed it in front of Harry Sr. She then said *"I hope you like it."* Harry Sr. devoured the food as if it was his last meal. Once again, Harry Sr. wiped his mouth on his t-shirt and then begged for more food.

Teasingly, Brenda moved the food trays away from Harry Sr. and said *"Not so fast. I have a favor to ask you?"* Harry Sr. looked at Brenda and said *"Ah, now I see what this is about."* After Brenda explained to Harry Sr. the favor she wanted him to do, he smiled and knew that he now had an opportunity to get more than what he actually deserved. He said *"Is this all I get?"* Eve and Brenda knew instantly that Harry Sr. was trying to sweeten the deal. Brenda easily read that so-called poker face she saw on Harry Sr.'s face and said *"Well, if you don't want this food, I guess I can give it to the homeless."* Harry Sr. looked at Eve and said *"This one has been hanging around you too much."* while pointing at Brenda. When he realized that Brenda was not joking about the food, he shook his head and told Brenda she had a deal. Brenda thanked Harry Sr. by giving him a kiss on his fore-head and immediately placed a large plate of food in front of him. She then said *"Enjoy."* Before Brenda left, Eve said to her *"Remember, don't bring him back."*

Anna and Bertha were not as fortunate as the rest of the ladies. After Brenda secured a deal with Harry Sr., they quickly found themselves out of options. Marty was in no way going to help any of the ladies especially since Cindy was on the warpath. Rick received a temporary restraining order forbidding him from helping the ladies during their quest. Harry had previously secured a deal with his wife. Since Anna and Bertha were out of options, they decided to help each other with the pranks but not with the individual stories. Thanks to Cynthia's restraining order, she was forced to solicit the help from one of our beloved pet characters.

Setting the Stage

At this point, I thought that everything had been set for the quest until I received a phone call from our third Judge. My friend was called away on an emergency and would not be available to judge our contest. I was at the coffee shop as usual when Beth walked in. I could sense that she wanted to give me her input on selecting a Judge. With a spring in her step, Beth approached the table and handed me a gift. It was a coffee cup from my "No Sense of Humor" collection. She said *"Hope you like it."* Beth didn't hesitate to ask *"So, have you found a Judge for the contest yet?"* Seeing right through her bribery attempt, I told Beth *"Nice try."* and handed her a folder. When she opened the folder, her eyes blossomed like a rose in the spring. Inside the folder was Beth's instructions as I selected her to be in charge of the contest as well as be our third Judge. I told Beth that since she did such a great job in organizing the beauty contest that she would be perfect for the job. All she had to do was monitor the ladies activities and progress of their stories, set up the event at the park and more importantly, keep the men away from the ladies. To her, it was a task easier said than done but after all, she is the writing assistant.

Beth knew that during the week prior to the contest that it was going to be extremely stressful for her. She had to contend with countless questions from the ladies regarding their stories. What she didn't anticipate were problems with two publishing companies that wanted bragging rights as well as exclusive rights to publish the stories from the contest and any stories that were written as sequels. Beth sent me a text message asking for my help. When I arrived at the store, I could see that stress had started to take its toll on Beth. She was sitting at her desk without any make-up on and her hair was so frazzled that it looked as if she was Wendy's twin sister. Trying to lighten the mood, I said to Beth *"Hi Wendy. Nice to see you again."* If only you could have seen the look Beth gave me. There was even a pencil stuck in her hair. After I saw the look and the mess she had created on her desk, I asked Beth how I could help her. She explained to me that Ralph's company and Eli's company wanted the rights to the stories but she couldn't make up her mind on who to choose. So, she asked the characters to come to the store for a sit-down and give Beth valid reasons why they should be selected.

This was one time I desperately wanted to call Cindy and have her bring her famous margaritas for Beth. Within moments, our famous characters walked in the door. They took a seat in front of Beth's desk. After the usual pleasantries were exchanged, Beth asked Ralph why his company should have the exclusive rights. He told the writing assistant that he had been the publisher since book two and deserved, or as he put it, earned the right to publish the stories. Eli told us that his company needed the stories since they had just started the business. He even pointed to the fact that he and Walter was forced to go straight. Beth looked at me and said *"See what I mean."* Beth was torn between her loyalty to Ralph but wanted to help Eli in establishing his business. I said to Beth *"I see your problem."*

I said to the gang *"Well, there is one way to settle this."* Ralph looked at Tom and said *"Don't worry. I am the Author's go-to canine. He will pick us."* The smug look on Ralph's face soon disappeared when I said *"Not so fast hot-shot."* I then told the so-called publishers that there should be a contest between the two and the winner will get the rights to the stories. Ralph said enthusiastically *"Yeah, let's have another snowball fight."* Eli wanted another wrestling match. Making sure that I did not give the edge to either team, I told the characters that they would be involved in a fishing contest prior to the start of the quest. The team who catches the most legal sized fish at the end of the trip would be declared the winners. Tom looked at me and said *"What trip?"* I told the gang that as a condition, they would have to spend the night together at the lake at the same campsite.

Since it was Thursday I told the beloved pets that I would take them to the camp site that afternoon. Their story at the lake would be narrated at the men's next poker night as a prelude to coming attractions. Tom gave me an evil glare and said *"What happens if we don't go along with this gag?"* I told the furry pet that I could always find another publisher. To add to the drama, I grabbed a phone book from Beth's desk and said *"Let's see........Oh, here is one. Jake's Publishing. I wonder if he is free this afternoon."* Ralph and Eli went home with their partners to pack for the trip. As soon as they left the store, Beth thanked me for my help. I told her that I was glad to help and smiled when we briefly discussed what could possibly happen at the lake. Yep, as you have read before, I always have to make another comment even though I don't have a sense of humor. Right as I opened the door, I turned to Beth and said *"By the way, nice hair style."* Luckily for me I was able to close the door before Beth could find an object that was capable of hitting its mark.

The Coveted Trophy

A VERY FISHY STORY

Remember when I said that it was going to be a very stressful week for Beth and the rest of the ladies? Well, according to the men at our next poker night, their week was just as stressful. We sat at the round table and all I could hear were the complaints from the men. Actually, the complaints only came from Marty and Rick. Harry and Harry Sr. were content as they had a wondrous week of pampering and fine food. Cindy spent countless hours in the den working on her story. She was so focused on winning that Marty ended up being her house servant, catering to her every need. Rick on the other hand did not have the luxury of having the same loving relationship Marty used to enjoy. Because of the restraining order, it put a damper on his social life. Actually, Cynthia posted a copy of the restraining order on one of his dating profiles. Rick brought the restraining order with him. Not sure if he wanted to brag about receiving one or if he wanted us to feel sorry for him. To me, this was the perfect time to make a copy of Rick's restraining order and place it on the wall at the shop.

I jokingly said to Rick as he dealt the cards *"Hey pal, four more restraining orders and you get a free set of steak knives."* Even Harry popped a comment to Rick. He pointed at the restraining order and said without a smile *"You want fries with that order."* After the laughter stopped I told the men that this poker night would only have one story that would be narrated. I told my comrades that this story was of our publisher's adventure at the lake. All the men gave me a look as if they were going to listen to a boring story. After all, there was one story previously written about Ralph and his family at the lake. Now it was my turn. I placed the story on the table and quickly commented on the use of pranks with a variety of novelties. Everyone except Marty was anxious to listen to the story. He said *"Might as well get this over with. At least this beats going home early and give Cindy another foot massage."*

Oh well, on with the story.

That Thursday at the office, my visit with Beth and the pet characters will clearly be remembered. Not just for what Beth was wearing that day in her glorious outfit but from what the pets perceived to be a potentially disastrous trip. Walter made the comment that he would have preferred surgery than spend a day at the lake with Ralph. While I waited outside the shop in my car, I could see Beth was still hard at work. I didn't dare enter the shop fearful that Beth would take the time to practice her throwing skills and use me as her target. While I was waiting for our beloved pets, I placed a well-intended phone call to Ben. I needed to make sure that he had the campsite ready for our arrival. Ralph and company returned with looks that were not deemed pleasant. After they loaded their gear, I took the pets to the campsite and told them that I would pick them up Friday morning. *"I have a surprise for you"* I said to the gang and then handed each of them the rules of the contest along with a letter of introduction from the new campsite director.

I drove off knowing that my beloved pets were in very capable hands. While looking at the foursome through my rear-view mirror, I shouted out *"Play nice and don't let the bed-bugs bite."* Tom, still not grasping the use of those popular phrases said out loud *"Where is an exterminator when you need one."* At this point, the gang could only comment on the predicament they were in. Just as the gang separated themselves to find a spot to set up their tents, Ben arrived at the site. He arrived in a golf cart that displayed the new logo for the camp. Once he removed his sunglasses, Ben greeted his old friend Ralph. He said *"Hey pal. Nice to see you again. Hope you like what I've done to the place."* Ralph said to his old friend *"Ben, what are you doing here?"* The furry Raccoon told Ralph that I had him return for a story since the pets were involved in another camping trip. Ralph then glanced over his right shoulder and saw that the campsite was set up as the same as it was on a previous trip, fully equipped with outhouses. He then said to Ben *"Oh, I see now. This must be a prank set-up by the Author."* Ben assured Ralph and his merry gang that the Author did not plan any pranks.

The new campsite director went over the rules of the contest with the gang. Ben told the crew that they only had four hours of daylight left and suggested that they set up their tents later. First, Ben handed Ralph a map of the location for their fishing spot. He then handed Eli a map which gave the location for their spot that was marked on the other end of the lake. Ben then told the gang that they had to report to the weigh station once it got dark to weigh in any fish that they caught. He also told the gang the Game Warden would be monitoring the event to make sure everything was done legally and according to the contest rules. Ben returned to his golf cart and eagerly said as he was leaving *"See you at the weigh station."*

Once Ben was out of the site, each team spent a few moments going over their location and plan. They wished each other luck and both teams bragged about how they were going to win the contest.

Team Ralph was the first team to embark on their mission. Ben secured a great location for the team. They were allowed to fish the docks nearest the marina. Two foot bridges connected to the marina made it a great location to cast without the interference of on-lookers or jet skiers. There was even a picnic table set up for the canines which served as a break area. In essence, that area was also reserved as the weigh-in table for the contest. Ralph chose a secluded spot at the end of the docks nearest the road. This spot gave him the advantage to cast in many directions.

Tom went to the other end of the docks. His spot was more open since that part of the dock served as an entrance point to the cove. After several attempts of casting against the wind, Tom grabbed his tackle box and selected another spot near the center of the marina.

Tom set up his chair and quickly set his sights on a spot for his next cast. He jiggled the line in an attempt to entice the fish. Tom did this for several minutes and when he could not get a nibble, he set the pole down next to his paws. Just as Tom got comfortable in his chair, he noticed that his fishing line had a lot of slack in it. Tom picked up his pole and gently reeled in the slack. He then felt a quick tug on the line and saw the line go taut. Tom realized that he had a fish on the other end of the line and when he saw the line move to his left he raised the pole high in the air to set the hook. Excitement filled his body when he snagged a fish. Tom yelled to Ralph *"Ralph, come quick. I need your help. I bagged one."* Ralph rushed to the aid of his partner. Together, they attempted to reel in the fish that Tom had snagged. After a few exhausting moments, the line went slack once again. At first, Tom thought that his potential keeper got away. It was at this point Tom and Ralph should have stayed focused on the job at hand. Tom frowned and reeled in the remaining slack from his line. Just as he was about to place his pole down in disgust, the line to his pole went taught once again. Ralph grabbed his partner and held on for dear life. However, the force from the other end of the line was so powerful that it pulled the duo into the water.

Tom could now get a first-hand look at the fish he had been wrestling with for the past hour. Staring at him was a large and I mean very large Catfish. Its mouth was so big that it was about to swallow Tom whole. Tom said to himself *"Holy crap."* His whole life flashed before his eyes. Now he knew what it was like being on the other end of the pole. Just as he was about to be swallowed whole, the Game Warden reached into the water and pulled the duo to safety. Tom said to the Warden *"Thanks pal. For a moment there I thought I was going to be fish food."* The Warden replied *"You are welcome. We are here to serve and protect."* After giving Tom and Ralph a smile, the Warden pulled out a pad and began to write the duo a ticket. Ralph said to the Warden *"What's the ticket for? We almost got eaten by a fish."* The Warden finished writing the ticket and then pointed to the "No Swimming" sign that was posted on the dock.

Doing his best to control his temper, Tom looked at the Warden and said *"Dude, we were not swimming. The Catfish pulled us in. We were fishing."* After the Warden finished writing the second ticket, he handed it to Tom and said *"I see. May I see your license please?"* Tom shook his head at the Warden and said *"You know cats don't drive. Besides, he is the driver."* pointing to Ralph. The Warden explained to both Tom and Ralph that they needed to show their fishing licenses. Tom shrugged his shoulders and said *"Fishing license! What do we need another license for? They are just fish."* The Warden pulled out the state regulation for fishing and handed a copy to each of the so-called fisherman. He once again pulled out a pad and wrote another ticket. The young Game Warden tipped his hat at the duo and said *"Better luck next time."* As soon as team Ralph wiped themselves off and changed into dry clothes, they grabbed their gear and headed to the campsite. Ralph contacted Ben and told him of the event.

While Team Ralph took the long walk of shame back to the campsite, they hoped that Team Eli would have the same misfortune.

Eli and Walter stood at the edge of road observing the view of the cove. Ben picked an equally great site for Team Eli. In the middle of the cove stood a small platform. The dock was covered and gated but the pair noticed there were several spots along the dock that would be great to cast their poles. Off to their left was a beach area. This cove had appeared to be a bit wavy for fishing considering the amount of people Team Eli saw jet skiing in their area. So, even though the pair felt handicapped at this point, they were still bound and determined to win the contest. Slowly the duo made their way down the long narrow stairs to the dock. Walter picked the spot closest to the entrance to the cove. Eli selected a spot closest to the beach. For almost two hours, the pair sent out cast after cast with not so much as a nibble. Finally, Walter changed his spot and started to cast near the other end of the dock. Before he could cast his next throw, two jet skiers appeared out of nowhere and ran their skis close to Eli and Walter. Eli and Walter shook their fists at the skiers in protest. They certainly were not giving Eli and Walter the respect they deserved.

Walter said to himself *"Enough is enough."* and then told his partner *"Wait until the next skier tries that. I will show him."* Within moments, Walter rubbed his paws in anticipation as he saw his next victim. This one was a woman water skiing and wearing a very skimpy bikini. As the driver of the boat swung her in the direction of the cove, Walter said to himself *"I got you now."* He sent a cast spiraling in the direction of the young woman. When Walter saw that the hook attached itself to the back side of the woman's top, he gave a hefty tug as if he caught a keeper. Suddenly, the woman's top flew off her body as Eli witness his partner reel in the woman's bathing suit. Immediately the woman let go of the rope and covered herself. She emerged from the water outraged. On-lookers at the beach area came to the woman's rescue as one of the ladies placed a towel around the lady. The Game Warden heard the commotion at the beach and went to investigate. The woman told the Warden of what had happened to her bathing suit and didn't hesitate to point in Eli and Walter's direction.

After he explained to the young woman that he would investigate her complaint, he tipped his hat and headed in the direction of Team Eli. Walter saw the Warden approach the dock and said to himself *"Uh oh. This is not good."* Eli quickly went to his partner's aid and said *"Dude, what did you do now?"* Walter said *"Something that should have been done earlier."* He then reeled in his so-called prize and the pair found themselves staring at a bright, red woman's bikini top. Unfortunately for the duo that it was too late for them to hide the evidence. The Warden asked for an explanation as to how they came across the bikini top. Smiling, Walter told the Warden that his fishing pole got away from him. He also told the Warden that it was a new pole and he was trying to cast away from the wind when the woman approached on her skies. The Warden asked the pair for their licenses. Walter said to the Warden "*Sorry officer but we don't drive.*"

When the Warden asked the pair to see their fishing licenses, Eli looked at the Warden and said "*What fishing licenses? We don't need one. After all, we are former members of the Cat Mafia.*" Team Eli took out their old credentials and showed them to the young officer. Immediately the Warden busted out in laughter and then said to the pair "*Hey. That was a good one. I have not heard that one.*" He handed the credentials back to the pair, took out a pad and wrote each of them a ticket. The Warden then said "*Better luck next time.*" Eli and Walter could not believe they received a ticket. No one ever dared to go against the members of the Cat Mafia. Disgusted, they packed up their gear and headed to the campsite. Eli said to Walter while climbing the stairs "*Maybe Team Ralph had just as much bad luck as we did.*" and then added "*At least you got a souvenir.*"

Team Ralph was sitting quietly in their lawn chairs when Team Eli arrived at the campsite. Eli asked Tom why his team had returned early. Tom told his former henchmen that they had no luck and then went into story-mode on how he and Ralph were almost eaten by a Catfish. Walter similarly displayed his sense of humor when he showed Team Ralph his souvenir. He told Ralph *"I guess you can add it to your collection."* As nightfall approached, the teams gathered firewood so that at least they could enjoy the serenity of a peaceful campsite. It didn't take long for Tom to say *"So what do we do now?"* After several attempts by Eli and Walter to try and find a solution to their current problem, Ralph shouted that he had an idea. He mentioned that since the fishing contest was over that they should hold their own contest. Eli looked at Tom and said *"Has he been taking Prozac?"* while pointing to Ralph. Ralph also told the group that his plan would definitely make up for the lack of fish that should have been proudly displayed in their cooler.

Like always, Ralph took it upon himself to take the lead. Before he told the gang about the contest, he placed all of the lawn chairs side-by-side. He then went to each of the outhouses and taped a photo of the adult characters, mainly the men, to each outhouse. Ralph placed several lanterns by the outhouse to give the contest a more illuminating effect. Smiling like most canines would when they are about to have fun at someone else's expense, Ralph reached into his tackle box, pulled out Cindy's bra and attached it to his team's chairs. He then instructed Eli and Walter to do the same to their chairs. Ralph pulled out a bag of balloons and instructed his pals to fill the balloons with water. As a nice little twist, Ralph prepared a special dye mix that was added to the water. He said to the gang *"We each take turns tossing the balloons at the targets using the bras. Each team will get four shots. The team who hits the targets in the face area the most wins the contest."*

Considering that fishing was not going to be used to see which team had bragging rights, the gang felt that this new contest would be the only way they could find out who was the better team. With music blaring in the background, the teams took turns tossing their balloons. Ralph went first and zeroed in on his target; Marty. He yelled *"Fire away."* and sent the first balloon to its intended target, hitting the Marty photo right on the nose. Score one for Team Ralph. Tom took his turn and aimed a different colored balloon at his favorite target; Rick. Just like his partner he yelled *"Fire away."* as he sent his balloon toward his target. Unfortunately for him, the balloon landed short and splattered on the ground. This gave a chance for Team Eli to win the contest.

After placing the balloon in the improvised sling-shot Walter made, Eli turned to his partner and said *"Watch this."* Eli took careful aim and sent the balloon to its intended target; Harry Sr. Team Eli jumped for joy when they saw the balloon hit Harry Sr. on the fore-head. It was now up to Walter to claim the bragging rights for his team.

Meanwhile, several campers nearby had been trying to sleep. The music that came from the gangs' campsite was too loud for them to bear so they contacted the Game Warden to see if he could put a stop to it. He knew which campsite to investigate since two of the gang members were privileged to receive tickets from him earlier that day. With a flashlight in one hand and a pad in the other, the Game Warden approached the gang and said *"I should have known it was you two."* as he looked at Eli and Walter. Walter had already been at the ready-line with his balloon neatly tucked in the bra. The tall figure startled Walter so much that he lost his grip on the bra. He said to himself *"Oh crap."* As the balloon whistled straight into the air, all eyes followed the balloon as it then hit its target. Luckily for the Game Warden the balloon splattered on his hat. Without hesitation, the Warden wrote two more tickets. After he handed them to Eli and Walter, Eli said to the Warden *"What are these for?"* Once again, the Warden tipped his hat and said *"For disorderly conduct and disturbing the peace."*

As the Warden left the campsite, Eli turned to his partner and said *"You know, he reminds me of the Author."* When Walter asked his partner how, Eli replied *"They both don't have a sense of humor."* Suddenly and without warning it started to rain. The gang realized that they forgot to set up their tents. As the rain poured on the furry pets, they finally managed to erect one tent. Content with having one shelter, the foursome placed their gear in the tent and decided to call it a night. It was raining so hard that Ralph made the comment *"Wow, it's raining cats and dogs out there."* Once again Tom did not understand those eloquent phrases. He peeked his head out of the tent and said *"I hope it's none of my friends."* For the next two hours it rained so much that the gang could see the water build-up on the top of the tent. When the rain stopped, the gang was able to fall asleep.

It didn't take long before the group woke up to the noises of the wilderness. Tom rose from his sleeping bag and said *"What was that?"* Ralph said *"Probably nothing, now go back to sleep."* A few moments later Tom heard the same noise. He said for the second time *"What was that."* After being hit in the head with several pillows, the rest of the gang told Tom to go back to sleep and that it was only his imagination working overtime. Tom laid back down still thinking there was something or someone near the tent. He said to the gang *"Didn't Ben tell us that there were Black Bears in the area?"* Silence from the gang was not what Tom wanted to hear. He said to himself *"If I wanted to get eaten alive, I would have let that Catfish do it."* Suddenly, the rest of the gang woke up when they heard a rustling sound that came from the back of the tent. As soon as the noise reached the side of the tent, Tom said *"See, I told you something is out there."*

When Ralph grabbed a flashlight and a bat, Tom said to him *"Oh now you believe me."* The noise coming from the side of the tent got louder. Shaking, Eli said to Tom *"You are the former Cat Mafia leader, go check it out."* As the pair bantered on who should be the one to check out the noise, Ralph pointed the flashlight at the side of the tent. They could make out a small silhouette. Suddenly a large roar echoed through the campsite. When the foursome heard a second roar, the side of the tent started to collapse when something tore through the canvas. Scared beyond belief and afraid that they were going to be eaten alive, Ralph yelled *"Let's get out of here."* Both teams ran out of the tent and quickly found refuge to the only shelter they could find; the outhouses. What seemed like an eternity, the group waited patiently to see if their so-called intruder left the campsite.

Not hearing any noises, Ralph decided to try his bravery and check to see if the intruder left the campsite. He tried to open the door to his outhouse but found out it was jammed on the outside. Ralph made several attempts to open the door but with no luck. He yelled out to the rest of the gang to see if they had the same problem. Tom yelled out *"Mine is jammed too."* When they all realized that they were trapped in the outhouses, they screamed at the top of their lungs for help. I think it was safe to assume that since the group had a previous complaint against them about noise that there was not going to be any help. It was not until daybreak that they got rescued. Ben arrived in time to save the day. He opened the door to the outhouse that Ralph was in and said *"What are you guys doing in these outhouses."* Ralph quickly opened the remaining doors and told Ben *"You are not going to believe what happened to us."*

I picked up the teams that Friday morning anxious to hear who won the fishing contest. I looked at Ralph and said *"So partner, who won the contest?"* Neither one of the pets could muster an answer. All I saw were four pets sitting in the back seat of my car with their paws crossed giving each other disgusted looks. Once again I looked at Ralph and said *"Must have been one heck of a contest."* As we were leaving the campsite, I noticed the Game Warden was standing on the side of the road, almost in a similar spot that Ben had once stood when the adult characters were on their camping trip. He waved at us as we passed the exit to the campsite.

At least the pets got a first-hand look at what camping was all about. After taking the characters home, I went to the office to give Beth the results of the contest. Beth was in a cheerful mood when I walked in the door. She even changed her outfit and looked more refreshed than the day before. I asked Beth *"So, what kind of an evening did you have?"* Beth smiled and several times batted her eyes at me as she told me a story of the eventful night she had. I looked at Beth and said *"Really, sounds kind of fishy to me."* Sensing that I was on to her, she said *"It's true. I had a marvelous evening."* Her smile told me otherwise. As she left her desk to attend to another matter, I noticed that the bottom draw to her desk had something that was sticking out of it while it was closed. I reached down to open the draw and when I saw the item I said to myself *"Well I'll be."* Inside the draw was a tape-recorder, a fake Bear claw and a uniform. The uniform was that of a Game Warden. I said to myself *"Yes Beth, very fishy indeed."*

NOVELTIES R US: REVISED

Marty looked at his watch and said to me *"Please tell me you have another story."* I told Marty that there was only one story scheduled. The rest of the men looked at each other to see if anyone could come up with a story. It was too early for the men to go home. Harry Sr. Said *"Well, it was fun while it lasted."* as he finished the last plate of lasagna. For me, I didn't want the evening to end so I said *"Wait. I have an idea."* I placed a catalog on the table and then added *"Care to have some fun?"* Marty's eyes widened when he picked up the catalog and said *"Wow. I can't believe you kept it after all this time."* It was the original catalog that was first mailed to Sophie that listed the original novelties. *"Speaking of novelties"* was what I blurted out to the gang when I placed another catalog on the table. This one was a new and improved catalog called the "No Sense of Humor" catalog. Ralph created the catalog to help increase sales at the store. Not only did this catalog list the old novelties, but it also displayed all of the new and improved novelties with suggestions for their use.

Harry Sr. peered through the pages of the catalog and pointed to several items that he thought were amusing. When I told Harry Sr. about the items and how they were used in the series, he said *"I can't wait to hear this."* So, for Harry Sr.'s benefit I decided to tell him the glorious uses of our novelties and how they were used.

In the beginning there were three items that I had selected as novelties to be used by the characters for their pranks. First was the Glow in the Dark Toilet Paper. This novelty has numerous uses. What makes this novelty unique is the glow in the dark particles that are embedded in the rolls. A person can buy them in bulk or in single rolls. They come with a full set of instructions as well as a disclaimer in case of excessive use. I looked at Marty and smiled when I made my next comment. I said *"In other words, if you decide to sit on the throne all day, your butt will light up like a Christmas tree in Time Square."* Marty may have remembered that famous quote from book one but Harry Sr. wanted to know the story. I told him that when the original catalog was given to Cindy, she wanted to order an item to play a prank on Marty. The Glow in the Dark toilet paper was first introduced at a dinner party Cindy held at her house one evening. It was a staged event so to make a long story short, Marty's butt glowed in the dark for several days.

Since that glorious evening, the Glow in the dark toilet paper was used quite extensively. In fact, I was the brunt end of a Cindy joke when I used the toilet paper in her bathroom one day. In the story "Marriage: No Way Out", Cindy forgot to place guest towels in her bathroom. I decided to use the toilet paper to wipe my hands and face not realizing that Cindy forgot to change out the rolls. I emerged to great her guests glowing in the dark. What made the evening more amusing for the gang was that I had a date planned with a very beautiful woman that night. Marty said *"Oh yeah. I remember that."* and then added *"If Zeke would have been around for the first book, you two could have passed as brothers."* Rick wanted to add to Marty's merriment and said to me *"By the way, did you go on that date?"* Without smiling, I told the men no. Harry asked me why so I took a long sip of my drink, swallowed my pride and said to the men *"Because she joined the convent."* Once the laughter stopped, I told Harry Sr. that a new novelty was created from the Glow in the Dark Toilet Paper. Glow in the Dark Paper Towels were used in a variety of stories that were also used by the pet characters.

I told Harry Sr. that his favorite pet character Ruby made the use of the towels famous in the story "Camping Canines." In that story, Ruby took it upon herself to teach her brothers a lesson and placed glowing towels and toilet paper in the outhouses at their campsite. According to her, revenge was sweet when she posted photos of her brothers in their school newspaper. Since then, Ruby has earned the respect of her brothers. She earned more respect as the queen of pranks by the canines in the story "Fashion Foes" from book five. Marty said with fake tears *"I am so proud of her."* In that story, Ruby wanted to pull a prank on Elizabeth's prissy canines, Princess and Queenie. Even though the prank back-fired, it was still successful considering the prank ended up being played on Elizabeth.

When I told Harry Sr. that the glowing towels and toilet paper was first played on Bertha, he said *"Wow. That woman scares the crap out of me."* We all remembered that eventful evening. It was an evening that not only allowed us to display the use of our novelties to children but to help the nurses teach Bertha a valuable lesson. It was that story "To the Hospital We Come" that became famous and is currently used as a guide by nurses around the country. Even the female adult characters got a first-hand glimpse of the glowing towels in the story "Epic Summary" from book four. The ladies that evening were forced to dive into the duck pond. On the other side of the pond, Sophie had created a drying station that was actually used in a previous story but never taken down. The glowing towels just sat on the table waiting for unsuspecting victims.

The next novelty I showed Harry Sr. was unique in itself and certainly was an item that got a lot of us in trouble. Yep, I am talking about the Man in the Box. I first found this item in a catalog while I was visiting an old friend. This box replicated a closed crate and created a sound through voice or noise activation. Every time someone would make a loud noise or even clap their hands, it would activate the voice inside the box as it would say *"Let me out, let me out."* The Man in the Box could be used almost anywhere as I am sure that Rick and Harry could attest to. It even got me in trouble with the Police in the story "Judgment Day" from book one. In that story, Sophie and I were taking a ride in my car when the Police pulled me over. Harriett had given me a package earlier that day in which I set the package in the back seat of the car, unaware that the Man in the Box was in the bag. While I was talking to the Police Officer, the noise activated the Man in the Box. The officer thought I was making disrespectful comments so he wrote me a ticket in which I had to go to court.

I looked at Harry and said *"Remind me to thank your wife for that."* He looked at me and said *"Hey, don't blame Harriett, blame him."* as he pointed to Rick. Yep, Harry was right. It was all Ricks fault. In the first book, Rick decided to play a prank on Harry. He placed the Man in the Box under Harry's bed one day. Harry on previous poker nights had bragged to the gang about his escapades in the bedroom with Harriett. One night Harriett was so involved that the noise that emanated from the bedroom could certainly classify as a break in the sound barrier. One could only imagine what Harriett thought when she heard the words *"Let me out. Let me out."* Love making would certainly take on a whole new meaning. Mr. High Pockets received a lesson from Harry in the story "Basic Training for Dogs". As you all know, certain dogs are known for their barking. To cure Mr. High Pocket's problem of excessive barking, hence his nickname the "Yapper", Harry placed the Man in the Box inside his beloved pets crate hoping that would end the countless hours of barking.

Harry had hoped that his beloved pet at the time would lose his voice after barking at the box for several hours.

Last, but not least, there were the His and Hers remote controls. I looked at Harry Sr. and said *"You remember those, don't you?"* Harry bought his parents a set of these remote controls one year as a Christmas gift. These remotes are not what you would consider useful to turn on and off certain appliances. They contained special buttons for pleasure and when pointed at a specific gender, the red light on the remote would be activated. There were buttons for food, sleep, sex and even displayed a mute button. Harry Sr. threw away the remotes when he claimed that they did not work. According to him, when he pressed the mute button and aimed the remote at his wife, she continued to talk. Harry Sr. said jokingly *"Next time get me a Parakeet."* This novelty has not been used since.

"Out with the old and in with the new." I said to the gang as I started on my quest to discuss the uses and history of the new novelties. Rick suddenly shouted *"Wait."* He wrote something on a piece of paper and taped it to the outside of my front door. Curious, I looked at the sign and it said *"Do not disturb. Men hard at work."* Maybe this will convince you that I still don't have a sense of humor.

History of the Bra

What can you say about a bra? Woman view the use of a bra as a necessity, a much-needed commodity that is used to improve their appearance. As far as the men and the pet characters are concerned, the use of a bra has a different meaning all-together. Marty was the first to create the idea that a bra has other useful purposes. One day when he was reviewing the catalog, Marty was looking for straps for his lawn chairs. He wanted to see if he could find a way to add cup holders to the chairs. For several days the notion of a lack of cup holders bothered Marty. He found a solution to his dilemma when the adults went on their first camping trip. Once Marty set up the chairs, he looked around for straps and cup holders. This was one time he wished he would have gone to the store before the trip. While he was in the tent searching for straps, Marty came across Cindy's bra. He attached the bra to the chairs with the cups facing upward making an improvised cup and beer holder. In a sequel story called "The "F" Word", Marty used two bras on another camping trip, both filled with ice and beer.

Ralph and company knew of Marty's exploits with the bra and decided to use them to their advantage. In the story "Psycho Kitties" from book two, Cindy's bra became a trademark when the canines used the bra to defeat the cats in their classic snowball fight. They were used once again in the story "Psycho Kitties: The Sequel". In that story, Tom was the leader of the Cat Mafia and stole the bras in an attempt to defeat the canines. Had it not been for the intervention of Mr. High Pockets, the cats would have had their first victory over the canines. Cindy's bra was mentioned again during the famous beauty contest when one of the contestants appeared before the men with her bra exposed and had a beer bottle expertly placed in the center of the bra for everyone's viewing pleasure. Today, Ralph proudly displays Cindy's bra at the novelty shop, under lock and key.

The Famous Flame-Thrower

What started out as a toy gift for Mr. High Pockets, the flame-thrower evolved from countless stories that would portray Mr. High Pockets as a canine celebrity. When Harry first adopted Mr. High Pockets, he found that his beloved pet had a fixation for guns. This came about from the extensive training the "Yapper" received at Camp Paws due to his anger issues. For days Mr. High Pockets would stand in front of Daisy Mae and pretend to shoot Harriett's prize bird with his six-shooters. When the "Yapper" found that the six-shooters were getting him nowhere, he decided to improve his marksmanship by using Harry's hunting rifles. Luckily for Harry, he found out about Mr. High Pocket's intentions and replaced the rifles with water pistols. It wasn't until the story "Only In the Movies" that the flame-thrower was used as what it was intended for. Mr. High Pocket's was working as a counselor at Camp Paws at that time. One of his duties was to run the canines through an obstacle course. One day, he decided to add realism to the obstacle course and used the flame-thrower as an enticement for the canines to complete the course. In that story, Mr. High Pockets accidently dropped the flame-thrower and when the gun hit the ground, it sent a barrage of fire in the direction of the camp's mess hall burning it to the ground.

After the incident at Camp paws, I decided to modify Mr. High Pocket's weapon by converting it to a water pistol. This modification did not change the "Yapper's" approach to its use. In the story "The Therapy Session" from book three, Mr. High Pockets used the flame-thrower to shoot the therapist but only with water. Even Pixy and Dixy got in on the act and used Mr. High Pocket's old six-shooters and also shot the therapist, this time with strawberry jam. In book four, the "Yapper" took a break from using his trusted gun. For the story "The Introductions", Mr. High Pockets made a sad attempt to impress a young child with his twirling skills. He lost control of the guns and when the six-shooters hit the table, the guns went off and sent an array of shots of strawberry jam at the Director of the Library. Needless to say that her white blouse was ruined. Now you know why the sub-title for book four was called "What Was I Thinking".

In book five, I thought that Mr. High Pockets had learned his lesson. Using the flame-thrower only got him in trouble. There was no good use for the gun. However, Mr. High Pockets was not about to be discouraged by a few mishaps. In the story "All in a Day's Work", the "Yapper" made a modification of his own. He now had the option to shoot water and foam. Mr. High Pockets was hired by the Director of the Vet Hospital to oversee the day-care center for canines. One day he decided to use the flame-thrower and put the canines through an obstacle course similar to the one used at Camp Paws. This course would be different. Mr. High Pockets used his gun to give the canines a bath. As luck would have it, the gun jammed and all he could see was that the entire Vet Hospital became flooded. This was the second job the "Yapper" was fired from.

Mr. High Pockets was not the only canine that got in trouble when the flame-thrower was used. In the story "Training the Protégé's: Return to Camp Paws", Bruce used the flame-thrower to teach certain canines a lesson. During their brief stay at the camp, Lilly was bullied by two canines when she was about to participate in the obstacle course. Being the protective brother that he was, Bruce singed the hair off the canine's back. When the head counselor shouted to Bruce, it startled the young canine so much that he dropped the flame-thrower. As in previous stories, the flame-thrower once again sent a barrage of fire towards the new mess hall. Luckily for me I am still on good terms with the Director of Camp Paws. I think that a generous check and a letter of apology from the canines helped.

The only time I thought that Mr. High Pockets used the flame-thrower for a useful purpose was in the story "Fashion Foes". That was one of Ruby's prank stories to seek revenge on Elizabeth's precious canines. It was an event in which the Mayor attended. During the event, the Mayor lost his footing and slipped on a pile of fake dog-poop. His toupee fell to the ground. When one of Ruby's brothers yelled "*Rat.*", Mr. High Pockets emerged from the kitchen eager to save the day. When he saw the toupee on the ground, the "Yapper" shouted his famous command and burnt the toupee beyond recognition.

Remember when I stated that Ralph wanted to have fun with Cindy's bra. Now it was the adults turn to have a crack at the popular novelty. Cindy was the first female character to use the flame-thrower in the story "The Pool Party: A Murder Mystery". She invited the canines to her house to solve a murder mystery. When she found out that the men replaced one of the canine characters with Max, Cindy became furious and decided to teach the men a lesson. This was after she found out that the men had set up a station near the back yard. Cindy donned Max's costume and equipped with the flame-thrower, approached the men. As the men saw Cindy remove her disguise and aimed the flame-thrower in their direction, the men got scared and took off running. Cindy got her satisfaction when she sent several shots of liquid dog-poop in the direction of the men all of which hit its target. Prior to that incident, Mr. High Pockets, or whoever was disguised as the "Yapper", fired the flame-thrower inside Cindy's house. It didn't take long for her to see that her walls in the living room were covered with strawberry jam. I felt sorry for Cindy that evening not because of the pranks that were pulled, but because Cindy had the walls re-painted just hours before the party.

Since Cindy liked the use of the flame-thrower, she used it to her advantage when she tried to have Mr. High

Pockets pull a prank on Beth when she was introduced as the new writing assistant. In the start of book seven, Cindy and the rest of the ladies were jealous of Beth and came up with an idea to force her to quit. Cindy solicited the aid of Mr. High Pockets. The "Yapper" once again used his trusty flame-thrower to rise to fame. Even though Beth was the intended target, Marty and Harry ended up being the brunt end of Cindy's prank.

Using Mechanical Pets

Mechanical pets used in the "No Sense of Humor" series were created to enhance specific story-lines, at least not in the traditional sense. Yes, there are mechanical pets that are bought and sold in stores that are voice activated and some come with remote controls. But our mechanical pets were developed with a specific personality in mind and evolved as the series grew. The original use of the mechanical pets came from an idea Marty had in attempting to solve a unique problem. He placed a tin can on a stick and painted the can to look like a cat. A tail was attached so that when someone or something tugged on the tail, it would activate a device inside the head so that the cat could speak. From that point on, mechanical pets were created that not only enhanced the story-line but were used for more than just a prank on an unsuspecting victim.

In the original story "Psycho Kitties", Ralph used a mechanical bird to replicate Daisy Mae to foil the attempted kidnapping of Harriett's bird by the Cat Mafia. Harry used a similar mechanical bird in the story "The Replacement" to foil another plot but intended to pull a prank on Mr. High Pockets. The first use of a mechanical canine was created in book two's story "Prisoner Exchange" where Sophie used a replica of Snowball to rescue her friend from a dog prison. Sophie dressed up as a pregnant canine and smuggled the mechanical pet under her blouse into the prison. Improvements were made on the mechanical canines by adding sounds and having devices installed so that the mechanical pets acted and performed in the same manner as their counterparts. This came about in one story called "The Exclusionary Rule" during a fashion contest in which mechanical canines were used to sabotage a fashion show. These canines were equipped with special scented liquid dye packs that when displayed on contact, they would look, smell and feel like real dog-poop all from a touch of a button.

Book four saw extensive use of mechanical pets in the stories created and narrated by the children. The first use of a mechanical chimp was used in the story "Monkey Business". Here, a mechanical chimp was used to replace Max so that he could have his freedom. There was one story in which Ralph and Tom were directed by me to work together. For "Show and Tell", Ralph and Tom got duped by a mechanical cat as they found themselves locked in a crate that was originally designed to catch a mechanical cat. The first mechanical canines that were used as a decoy for another prank saw plenty of action in the story "Cruising Critters". A water slide had been built under the platform where the mechanical canines had been stationed. When one of the canine's tails was moved, it would activate the water slide and anyone who stood on the platform found themselves in a spiral downward slide into the duck pond. Sophie and Jack were privileged to enjoy that station during their date in the park. Even the female adult characters got involved one evening. Not soon after the children's' scavenger hunt, Marty took the ladies on a romantic tour of the park. The majority of the stations that had been set up for the hunt were still displayed. Curiosity got the better of the ladies as they wanted to know what the children went through while on their scavenger hunt.

Darlene and Sophie made the use of mechanical canines popular in their story from book four called "You Know What." Since the Cat Mafia had taken sides with the Boy Scouts, Darlene felt it necessary to even the odds. Together, she and Sophie obtained almost a dozen mechanical canines that replicated German Sheppard's. They figured that the size of the canines alone would make the Boy Scouts leave them alone. It certainly put a lot of fear into the Cat Mafia. The use of a mechanical Rabbit was first thought of by Darlene in a rescue story called "Its Magic Time". Randy was kidnapped during the magic show at the hospital and was sent to the same prison that Snowball had been sent to. Darlene used the mechanical Rabbit in the same manner Sophie used Snowball during their prisoner exchange. Another mechanical Rabbit was used to bail out the First Dog in the story "Canines and Politics: Part Two". With the aid of Zeke, Mr. High Pockets created a mechanical Rabbit to show that George was not the kind of replacement suitable to take over the position as First Dog.

Fake Beehives

This novelty was first introduced by Marty's dad. Martin was a prankster that lived up to his reputation for being one of the cleverest pranksters in the business. He gave the gang a preview of the fake beehive one day at the park. The features alone made the item appear to be real. What made this novelty unique was that it was stuffed with candy. To add realism to the novelty, the fake beehive was attached with fake bees that contained sensors. As one would approach the fake beehive, the sensors activated the bees and suddenly one would hear the buzzing and grew louder as one got closer to the beehive. In many of the stories, the characters placed the fake beehive next to a real one.

There were two other novelties created in which one was deleted from the series for obvious reasons. Specially-ground coffee was another novelty Martin had introduced to the gang. The bag had the appearance of real coffee and even gave the scent of fresh-roasted beans. However, when the coffee was mixed with hot water, it gave the taste as that of horse manure. Since I am an avid coffee drinker, I am sure you can appreciate the humor in why I deleted that novelty. The other novelty was called the "Clacker". It was only used in two stories. Marty used it as a prank one evening to scare the ladies. He attached it to the toilet seat in his upstairs bathroom on a night the ladies were having their eventful night at his house. This device would be attached to the inside of a toilet cover. When someone lifts the seat cover, a loud and shrilling scream emanated from the device. The other was attempted on the men in a recent story as payback from the ladies. One new addition that expanded over the series was the creation of the "Bats". Several bats had been created to be used on certain characters. These bats not only contained an inscription of the name of the character but also embodied into the center of the bat was a photo of the character that it was to be used on. Bats that made the series famous were the "Marty" bats, the "Ralph" bats and the latest invention by Beth called the "Author" bat.

There was one novelty mentioned in book one that was not intended to be used in the series. It came about through an accidental swap. A friend of a friend met a beautiful woman one day at the Library. He invited her to his house for a night of romantic fun. When he realized that he was out of condoms, he called his best friend to purchase a box at the local drug store. His friend bought a box of condoms the day before from a novelty store that had been intended for a prank on another friend. This novelty contained a dozen condoms. They looked and were wrapped like real condoms but they were actually disguised as bubble gum. The friend accidentally left the novelty condoms in his apartment. To make a long story short, the friends pet came across the box of condoms and started to chew on them when the guy realized that he left the condoms in the living room while he was in the bedroom with the lady. Out of nowhere, the canine came into the bedroom with the box of condoms in his mouth chewing as if he had been given a treat. As the canine blew bubbles, the lady freaked out and left the apartment. In that story the canine did not have a speaking part. If he did, I am sure he would have said *"Hey dude, thanks for the treats. By the way, we are out of milk."*

Ray Gun

When a new character is introduced, sure and behold that a new novelty will soon follow. Creating Zeke as our favorite Alien was a welcomed addition along with his version of Mr. High Pocket's flame-thrower called the ray gun. For story purposes, the ray gun was equipped with selectors that were similar to the flame-thrower but built in a more stylish and powerful way. From what I can remember, the ray gun was used in three stories. In the story "Canines and Martians", Zeke used the new novelty to demonstrate its usefulness in a contest with Mr. High Pockets. The pair set up cans to be used as target practice. Zeke's ray gun was so powerful that it sent a smoldering can that engulfed the Canine Police sign. In a return story, the Zorba Squad used their improved ray gun to once again demonstrate its effectiveness by destroying a new sign that had been built by the Canine Police. Zeke even used the ray gun on Daisy Mae. Even though the ray gun was set to stun, it still gave Harriett a bad taste in her mouth with regards to Mr. High Pockets and his new best friend. The "Yapper" used the ray gun on his return trip to the White House. A special function built into the ray gun enabled Mr. High Pockets to zap George to keep him silent while giving the impression that the canine was still talking.

As soon as I finished my history lesson, Harry Sr. pointed to the ray gun in the catalog and said *"Wow. I need to get me one of these."* We all knew why Harry Sr. wanted the ray gun. To him, he would use it as a replacement for the remote controls. I gave each of the men a copy of the catalog and told them to enjoy it in good health. The men were just about to leave when suddenly there was a knock on my door. To our surprise, I received a singing telegram. It said *"Hope you boys had your fun as our quest for the title has just begun. In case you decide to order those items, you will all be in need of multiple vitamins. Signed, The Ladies."*

Cute but no cigar. Oh well, on with the quest.

REVENGE OF THE PSYCHO KITTIES

After I read the prelude to coming attractions regarding the ladies quest for the tile, I thought to myself *"I sure hope that the men behave."* When I arrived at the park, Beth was busy setting up the Judge's table. I looked around and saw that Beth did a marvelous job setting up the area for the contest. She set the Judge's table in front of the gazebo and on each side of the Judge's table Beth placed a row of chairs for our beloved observers. To the right was the section for our pet characters and to our left was the station for the men. Another row of chairs were set up for the ladies to sit while they viewed the contest. Yep, my writing assistant once again did a fabulous job. A beautiful Saturday in the park. The sun shone bright, the birds chirped in harmony and Ducks gracefully enjoyed the pond. To me, it couldn't have been a more picture-perfect event.

The ladies arrived without the men. At first I thought it was strange that the ladies arrived together and in the same vehicle. But after all, the ladies were close to one

another and considered each as part of the family. To them,
why let a simple contest ruin their friendship. According
to Cindy, that's what husbands are for. When the men
arrived, their jovial spirit was not enjoyed by the ladies
as I saw the ladies greet the men with sheer silence as
well as their arms crossed. Ralph and the rest of the pets,
mainly the publishers, arrived still upset from their latest
quest. They were told by me that their presence was just
for support. Beth and I took our positions at the Judge's
table. I could hear the men bantering in the background.
Adam arrived and took his position at the Judge's table.
When he placed the bottle of Scotch on the table, Marty
whispered to Rick *"That should be our bottle."* Finally, we
were ready to start the contest. Beth stood to introduce the
participants and after she went over the rules of the contest,
our first contestant approached the Judges table. Harriett
was selected to go first since she was the reigning queen.

Harriett smiled as she handed each of the Judges her
story. Before Beth and I could commence the start of the
contest, we suddenly heard music coming from the far
end of the park. A band appeared and played music as
if they were paying tribute to a celebrity. I should have
known better when I saw Mr. High Pockets emerge from
the crowd with photographers and reporters close at hand.
After waving to the crowd, he took his seat with the rest of
the canines. For several minutes Harriett gave Mr. High
Pockets an evil glare. I could tell that the look she gave
the "Yapper" made his hair stand straight in the air. When
Harriett decided that her look had now served its purpose,

she placed a small statue of Mr. High Pockets on the Judge's table. It appeared to be a small cookie jar. I asked Harriett what the jar was for. She jokingly replied *"To put Mr. High Pocket's ashes in when I am done with the story."* After I said *"I see."* I told Harriett that she may now begin her story and flipped the hour glass. According to Harriett, this was her story called "Revenge of the Psycho Kitties".

One Saturday Harry had just finished his latest project in the basement when Harriett called for him. He had been working so hard that Harriett took it upon herself to treat her husband to lunch at their favorite diner. While they were at the diner, Harriett started the conversation regarding their new neighbor and asked her husband if he had a chance to meet her. Startled, Harry said to his wife *"I didn't know we had a new neighbor."* He then added *"Remember what happened the last time we had a new neighbor?"* Harriett told her husband that their new neighbor was different and not involved with the Cat Mafia. She told Harry that their neighbor was married and that her husband was stationed overseas. Harriett said *"That poor woman. Being all alone like that. You should help her sometime."* She also added that their neighbor owned cats as well as a prized African Parrot that her husband bought her for their anniversary. Harry then asked his wife *"By the way, what is her name?"* As soon as Harriett said the name Annie, Harry spit out his food and shouted *"Annie."*

Harry looked at his wife and said *"Do you know who that woman is? She is the co-leader of the Cat Mafia."* Harriett said *"Don't be silly. Besides, she told me all about those dreadful stories you men created about her."* She then added *"You men will do anything for a story."* Harry once again looked at his wife and said *"Dear, you are so naïve."* The couple finished their meal and headed home. When they arrived at the house, the couple saw Annie mowing her front yard. Harriett waved to Annie and then told her husband that he wanted him to be on his best behavior that night since she invited Annie over for dinner. Harry went to the basement to start in his next project. He said to himself that he needed to figure out a way to convince his wife that Annie was nothing but trouble. Harry came back to the kitchen and told Harriett that he needed to go to the hardware store and buy more blades for his table saw. As soon as he was out of the house, Harry called me and said that he had a problem and wanted me to meet him at the coffee shop.

My coffee had just been delivered to the table when Harry walked in the shop. I could tell that he was nervous by the way he fiddled with his cell-phone. I asked Harry *"So, what's so important that would drag me away from work?"* Harry took a sip of his coffee and then told me about his new neighbor. Without pausing, he said *"Her name is Annie."* I asked Harry if he was sure it was Annie. He took out his cell-phone and showed me a picture that he took of a blond woman mowing the grass. I then said to Harry *"Yep, that's her alright."* At first, I told Harry that we were under the impression that Annie was in another country. So I called Samantha to check out Harry's story. She told me that she had not heard Annie was back in the country but would dispatch two of her agents to surveillance the house just in case. I then asked Harry what he knew about his neighbor. He said *"Just what Harriett told me."* As in a previous story, I wondered if Annie was plotting revenge to steal Harriett's bird. Harry told me that was unlikely since she owned her own Parrot. He then said *"Harriett invited her over for dinner tonight. What should I do?"* I told Harry to be himself and to get as much information as he could about Annie.

Harry walked in the front door waiting to see what else his wife would say about their neighbor. After he took the saw blades to the basement, Harry joined his wife in the kitchen to get more information out of her. Harriett said to her husband *"So why the sudden interest in our neighbor?"* Harry told his beloved wife that she was right. One should help someone who has a loved one that is serving our country. He then said *"Guess you can say it's the patriotic side of me."* Smiling, Harriett gave her husband a kiss on the cheek and told him that dinner would be ready soon. Harry went upstairs to change and said to himself *"Poor Harriett. She has no clue."*

When the door-bell rang, Harry knew it was their neighbor. Harriett greeted the blond with open arms. Annie brought a welcome gift to the party and handed it to Harriet. She said *"I hope you like it."* It was a photo of Annie's Bird. Annie then jokingly added *"I named him Harry."* Harry's mouth was wide open as he saw his wife and Annie start the evening with their version of man-bashing. Harriett quickly escorted Annie to the living room and poured each of them a drink. All Harry could do was listen to the gossip. He said to himself *"This woman is good."* After dinner, the conversation and gossip continued. In fact, Annie showed Harriett a photo album. For several minutes the ladies exchanged stories about their beloved pets. Just when Harry saw an opening for him to join the conversation, Annie shouted to Harriett *"I have an idea. Why don't we have a playdate for our pets tomorrow?"* Harriett was seen jumping up and down in her chair and told Annie that the playdate was a great idea. She even told Annie that at one point she was considering getting another bird for Daisy Mae to keep her from being lonely.

Once the evening was over, Harriett told her husband that she was heading to bed. It had been quite an exhausting day for Harriett considering she spent most of it cleaning the house and cooked a fabulous meal. As soon as Harriett was asleep, Harry called me. I asked Harry how the evening went and if he got more information about Annie. He said *"The evening went great. Harriett was happy but they gossiped all night so I couldn't get a word in edge wise."* Harry then expressed another concern when he told me that Annie and Harriett scheduled a playdate for their beloved pets the next day. I told Harry not to worry. He asked me if Samantha had any news about Annie and the Cat Mafia. I told my friend that there was no news from any of the agents. In addition, I told Harry that Harriett would make sure that nothing happens to her pet. The agents were still surveying the house and were there for back-up in case his wife needed help.

As Harry was about to hang up the phone, I could tell that he had another concern when he said "*Okay, but.....*" I asked Harry what else was on his mind. At first he said that it was probably nothing. But after a little prodding, Harry gave in and told me of the other concern he had. He said that Harriett had been overly protective of Daisy Mae ever since she found a necklace. Harriett one day took Daisy Mae for a check-up at the Vet. When she left the Vet's office, she noticed a piece of jewelry lying on the ground. Harriett thought that it was just a piece of costume jewelry for pets that someone probably threw away. She picked up the necklace and placed it around Daisy Mae's neck. Her beloved pet has been wearing the necklace ever since. I asked Harry "*Where is the Vet's office located?*" When he told me the address, I said shockingly to Harry "*Dude, your Vet's office is right next to Elizabeth's jewelry store.*" Suddenly, that proverbial red-flag popped up in both our heads. Harry said "*You don't think that the necklace is real do you?*" I told Harry that since the real necklace from the last jewelry heist had not been recovered that it was a possibility that it was indeed real.

Harry said "*I need to tell Harriett to cancel that playdate.*" I told Harry that he should let Harriett have her playdate. If our suspicions were correct, we can use the necklace to our advantage and have Annie arrested. Up to now, everything Harry told me was coincidental. It made a lot more sense knowing that this was possibly a plot by Annie to steal the necklace. My concern was trying to figure out how Annie knew that Daisy Mae's necklace was real. I told Harry that I would be at his house the next morning and together we would tell Harriett of Annie's true intentions.

In the meantime, Annie arrived at her house satisfied that phase one of her plan had worked. She poured herself a drink and shouted *"You can come out now."* Annie's top henchmen asked her *"How did it go?"* The co-leader of the Cat Mafia smiled and said *"Good. We have the playdate set for noon tomorrow."* She then took a fake necklace and placed it on her pet Harry. The necklace looked identical to the one Daisy Mae proudly wore. Annie then said to her henchmen *"Remember, as soon as we leave the room, make the switch."* Her plan was so good that Annie knew she would be out of the country by the time Harriett and company find out about the swap. She took another sip of her drink and said to herself *"Man, I hate dealing with those people."*

The next morning Harry opened the door before I had a chance to knock. He grabbed me by the arm and led me to the kitchen. He said *"We have to move fast. Harriett is getting ready to leave."* Harriett was in the kitchen putting dishes away when I walked in. She looked at me and said *"Hey dude, what brings you out on a Sunday morning?"* I told Harriett that Harry and I had something urgent to tell her. She looked at me and said *"If it's about Annie, I don't want to hear it."* Harry tried to get his wife to listen to reason and then said *"Come on dear, hear him out."* I then told Harriett that Annie was plotting to steal Daisy Mae's necklace. Harriett gave me a disgruntled look and said *"No way. Not that piece of junk."* When I told Harriett that the necklace might be one of the necklaces stolen from Elizabeth's collection, she said to me *"Yeah right. Like someone would leave a $100,000 necklace lying on the street."* Harry told his wife that there was one way to be sure. He said that if she would let a jewelry expert examine the necklace then that would prove that Annie is trying to steal the necklace. Harriett said *"No way am I letting a stranger near Daisy Mae. You two are definitely on Prozac."*

Harry and I made a few more attempts to reason with Harriett but she was bound and determined to go through with the playdate. I decided to stay with Harry until Harriett returned home to make sure her and Daisy Mae were safe. Samantha was contacted to inform her of the plan and to have her agents keep a lookout just in case. Harry looked at me and said *"Might as well relax. It's going to be a while."*

Annie just finished placing the snacks on the table when Harriett knocked on the door. She looked around to make sure her top henchman was out of sight. Satisfied that everything was in place, she opened the door and greeted Harriett with open arms. After she told Harriett about the brownies she had made for the occasion, Annie suggested that she and Harriett take Daisy Mae to meet her playmate. With enthusiasm, the ladies went to the den. Harriett placed Daisy Mae next to Harry. Annie said to Harriett *"See what I bought Harry."* pointing to the necklace her pet was wearing. She then told Harriett that she got the idea after her last visit with her. Annie then added *"Don't they look so cute together."* She then grabbed Harriett by the arm and said *"Let's leave them alone for a while so they can get acquainted."* The ladies returned to the living room to enjoy the brownies Annie made as well as gossip.

Almost two hours had gone by and not a word from Harriett. Harry was starting to get worried. He paced the floor hoping that he would soon get a call from his wife. The waiting and the anxiety was bothering Harry. I said to him *"Relax Harry, Harriett is fine. We would have heard from Samantha if there was any trouble."* Harry gave me a faint smile and once again looked at his watch. He said to me *"I can't take it no more."* and put on his jacket. I remembered the last time Harry felt like this. His beloved wife was kidnapped by the same organization. I grabbed my jacket and said to Harry *"Well, I am not letting you go alone."* Harriett opened the front door and had Daisy Mae with her when I had made that comment. Harry looked at his wife and said *"What took you song long? I was getting worried."* His wife said that they were so involved in gossip and man bashing that they lost track of time. I asked Harriett if Daisy Mae was okay. She said *"She is great. Look for yourself."* I inspected the cage and gave Daisy Mae the once over. Sure enough, not a feather had been ruffled and the bird still proudly wore the necklace. I looked at Harry and said *"Seems everything is okay."*

When Harriett left the room to put Daisy Mae in the den for her nap, she yelled out *"See, you two were worried for nothing."* She then whispered to herself *"Annie and the Cat Mafia. What will the men think of next?"* I called Samantha to inform her that Harriett and Daisy Mae were home safe and sound. She called off the agents since, according to her, it was a false alarm. Harry thanked me for my help and even offered to have me stay for dinner. Of course I accepted. It may not have been Eve's lasagna but it was definitely better than Sophie's cooking.

Annie saw the agents van that was parked across the street and left as soon Harriett had arrived home. She said to herself *"Morons. Who do they think they are dealing with?"* Yep, Annie knew all along that agents had camped out at her doorstep. She closed the blinds and told her henchman *"You can come out now."* Annie asked him if he made the swap and he replied *"Yep, like taking candy from a canine."* Annie took the necklace from the henchman and gently placed it in a velvet pouch and nestled it inside her bra. Yep, like it was said before a bra has a lot of useful purposes. Now that Annie had the necklace, she embarked on her final phase of her plan. Her intent was to sell the necklace and once she had the money in hand, use it to leave the country and join Amy.

On the other side of town was the pawn shop that the Cat Mafia had used quite extensively whenever they wanted to sell stolen goods. Annie walked into the shop and greeted the owner as if they were best friends. He said *"So my dear, what have you brought me this time?"* Annie's eyes widened in anticipation as she reached into her bra and handed the owner a velvet pouch. He then said to her *"Let's take a look."* The owner grabbed his eye piece and with expert hands placed the necklace on a cloth plate. At first glance he commented to Annie that it looked like a fine piece and then asked her how much she wanted for the necklace. She replied *"My sources told me that I should get at least $100,000."* The owner of the store turned on a lamp and examined the necklace. He looked at Annie and said *"That's an interesting piece of work you brought in."* Annie smiled and rubbed her hands counting in her mind the amount of money she was about to get. She said *"I know. When can I have the money?"* The owner pulled out a dollar bill from his wallet and handed it to Annie. She looked at the dollar bill and said to him *"Is this some sort of joke?"* Without smiling, the owner told her she brought in a fake. He even demonstrated its worth when he bit into the necklace. The owner handed the necklace back to Annie and said *"You can buy this necklace in any candy store for a dollar."*

At that point in time, we all wished we were flies on the wall. One could only imagine the explanative Annie used when she found out that the necklace was fake. Back at Harry's house, we were enjoying the evening with bantering and of course Harriett's cooking. Daisy Mae heard the commotion in the other room. She perched herself in the center of the cage and listened intently to the laughter. Daisy Mae smiled and said to herself *"Maybe one day they will realize that I am more than just a pretty face."* Safely tucked away under the newspapers that lined her bird cage was the real necklace.

Harriett received a standing ovation for her performance. Even the men did their version of the canine wave. She was then greeted by high-fives from the rest of the ladies. Harriett told the ladies that she would join them shortly. Seems that Harriett had unfinished business to attend to. Slowly she walked toward Mr. High Pockets. When Ralph saw the look Harriett was giving his pal, he whispered to the "Yapper" *"Dude. If I were you, I would run away and not look back."* Mr. High Pockets agreed with his friend. It was time for him to make a hasty exit but when he tried to stand up, he found himself glued to the seat. By this time Harriett was standing directly in front of Mr. High Pockets. She said to him *"I don't think you are going anywhere."* Harriett then opened the cookie jar she had proudly displayed earlier and poured its contents all over Mr. High Pockets. The poor "Yapper" was covered in honey. To add to his embarrassment, Harriett grabbed an open bag full of feathers and spread them all over his body. She said to Mr. High Pockets *"That's from Daisy Mae."* Harriett clapped her hands and joined the ladies. It didn't take long for the Duck caretaker to view the prank. The Duck waddled his way towards Mr. High Pockets. When he saw the mess, the Duck shook his head, looked up at the "Yapper" and said *"Sorry dude. I don't get paid to clean up this kind of mess."*

ATTACK OF THE ZORBAS

Our next contestant was not in a cheerful mood. Cynthia approached our table determined to win the contest. When she sat down, Cynthia gave Rick another evil glare. I whispered to Beth *"Is it too late to create another bat?"* Beth smiled at me and said *"Not at all."* She reached under the table and handed Cynthia the "Rick" bat. Without smiling, she once again turned to look at Rick while patting the bat in her hands. The canines liked what they saw and cheered for Cynthia by giving her a tribute mostly seen in sporting events; the wave. When the canines settled into their seats, I flipped the timer and told Cynthia *"You may now begin your story."* According to Cynthia, this is her story called "Attack of the Zorbas".

Zorba is a planet located light-years away from Earth. Aliens who live on that planet are rich in technology as well as their favorite pet. They are known to revere cats in such a manner that laws had been created on that planet to protect cats as if they were an endangered species. In fact, the Zorba commander received a cat as a gift and liked it so much that a name was chosen to show that the commander had a sense of humor, even though he didn't have one. Soon, citizens of the planet Zorba found new stores, hospitals and schools erected to honor their new pet.

Once upon a time, well, actually right before Zeke embarked on his latest adventure with Mr. High Pockets, he told the "Yapper" the history of his planet and more importantly how the Zorba commander got his name. To every Alien who revered and feared the commander, they called him "Z". One day the Zorba commander had participated in one of their game shows called "Spin the Zorba". After the commander spun the wheel to obtain more Zorba credits, he wanted to solve the puzzle but first wanted to buy a vowel. When the host told the commander that he did not have enough credits to buy a vowel, the commander took out his ray gun and zapped the host. Viewers on Zorba were shocked as the host of the show was now a pile of dust. The Zorba commander then went to the puzzle board and removed the only letter he could recognize; the letter "Z". Since that day, the commander proudly wears the letter "Z" on his shirt. He even had local Zorba stores make jackets and shirts with the newly acquired emblem. To protect his investment, the Zorba commander started a team that would protect the stores as well as collect protection money. Hence, the newly created organization became known as the Martian Mafia.

When Zeke returned home to his planet, he had found out that more stores were built with slave labor. One day Zeke walked into one of the Zorba stores to buy Zorba milk for his 227 children. He saw two Zorba gangsters talking to the owner of the store and overheard one of the gangsters force the owner to give him Zorba credits that are required for protection. As soon as Zeke heard another comment made by the other gangster, he followed the duo to find out what kind of plot they were involved in. Not to his surprise, Zeke saw the gangsters walk into the Zorba commander's office. Acting like a detective, Zeke pulled out his Zorba meter to listen to the conversation between the gangsters and the Zorba commander. He listened intently to the conversation. "Z" said to his men *"Now that we have enough protection credits, we can begin phase one of our operation."* The Zorba commander was then heard telling his men to gas up all available spaceships and be ready to start the invasion. Zeke said to himself *"What invasion?"*

Zeke moved the selector switch of his Zorba meter so that he could listen to the rest of the conversation. When he heard the words "Earth" and "Canines", Zeke became nervous and accidently dropped his Zorba meter. The loud thud Zeke created was heard inside the commander's office. One of the gangsters said *"What was that?"* and immediately drew his ray gun. "Z" told his men *"Go check it out."* As soon as the lead gangster opened the door, he found Zeke crunched down on the floor attempting to retrieve his Zorba meter. The gangster said to Zeke *"Well, well, well... If it isn't out little traitor Zeke."* Against his will, Zeke was escorted into the office. One of the gangsters said to "Z" *"Hey boss, look what we found."* and threw Zeke on the floor in front of the commander's feet. "Z" said to Zeke *"So, you were spying on us. I can fix that problem."* His men asked the commander what they were going to do with Zeke. "Z" replied *"Take him to the Zorba jail for now. We will zap him later after we get rid of those canines on Earth."*

Sitting quietly in his jail cell, Zeke had to figure out a way to contact his friends on earth about the invasion. He reached for his Zorba meter to contact the Canine Mafia but his device was damaged beyond repair. Zeke then thought to himself that his wife would try and contact him since he hadn't returned from the Zorba store. He pounded on the walls of his cell trying to get the attention of the Zorba guard but had no luck. The walls were virtually sound-proof. Zeke then tried telepathy to contact his wife but once again he failed. He paced the cell desperately trying to figure out a way to break out of jail. It was just a matter of time before the Martian Mafia would reach Earth and destroy the canines.

Meanwhile, back on planet Earth, Ralph and company were conducting their lives as normal as they could be. Ralph decided to walk to work one day. He passed one of the local pet stores and saw a sing hanging in the front window that displayed the words "Going out of Business Sale". Startled, Ralph walked into the pet store to see why the owner had displayed the sign. He had known the owner of the store for a long time and felt that this particular pet store would be the last one to go out of business. When Ralph greeted his old friend, he said *"I noticed your sign in the window. What's going on?"* The owner told Ralph that business was very slow and then told Ralph *"Take a look around."* Ralph noticed that the pet store displayed an abundance of cats, birds and fish but no canines. He asked the owner *"Where are all your canines?"* The owner told Ralph that he didn't know and further told him that he contacted all of his suppliers and that they were out of canines as well. It was as if the well had run dry. Ralph told the owner not to panic and that he would check it out. He then said to his old friend *"In the meantime, take down that sign. It's not over yet."*

Ralph walked into the novelty store still carrying that puzzled look. He saw Tom busy at his computer taking orders and Bruce hard at work taking calls for the Canine Mafia. It seemed to him that everything was normal so he grabbed his morning coffee and took a seat in front of Tom's desk. When Tom finished placing his last order, Ralph said to him *"You are not going to believe what I saw on the way to work."* Tom replied *"Okay Ralph, what is it? What joke do you want to tell now?"* Ralph told his partner that he saw a "Going out of Business" sign hanging in the front window of his friend's pet store. After explaining to Tom why his friend was going out of business, he asked *"Do we have that same problem at our pet shop?"* Tom told his partner that he didn't know so the two of them went to the pet store to make sure they did not have the same problem. Penny was working at the register when the duo walked in the shop. Tom asked his wife if she had any problems with acquiring canines for the store. She said *"As a matter of fact, two of our suppliers called and said that they would not be able to make this week's deliveries."* When Ralph asked her why, Penny replied *"Something about not enough canines to go around."* Tom looked at Ralph and said *"You don't think it's a coincidence do you?"* Ralph's eyes widened as he suspected that someone or something was creating a shortage of canines. To him, there was no such thing as coincidence.

When Ralph and Tom went back to the office, they called Samantha to see if she had word on the missing canines. She told the duo that she had received a lot of reports of missing canines but none of them were reported as kidnappings. Ralph then asked Samantha if she thought that Annie and the Cat Mafia might be involved. Samantha said *"Not that we can tell. Besides, she has been in another country for the last three days."* Tom then called Eli and Walter to see if they had any information on the lost canines. Through their contacts, the new publishers told Tom that the Cat Mafia was involved in another plot but had nothing to do with canines. As Tom got off the phone with Eli, Bruce came into Tom's office and said *"Hey dude, I am swamped."* He placed the message book on Tom's desk and told him that ever since they left, the Canine Mafia's phone had been ringing non-stop with calls about lost canines. Ralph said to himself *"If it's not the Cat Mafia, then who is it?"*

Since Ralph and Tom had no clue as to who was behind the canine shortage, they decided to close the business early and head home. Bruce returned to his work station to shut down the computers and then went outside for his last potty break. Ralph waited at Beth's desk while Tom locked up the novelty cases. Suddenly, Ralph heard a knock on the back door. At first he thought that Bruce locked himself out so he shouted to Bruce *"Hey Bruce, did you forget your keys again?"* When Ralph opened the door, he froze in his tracks motionless and speechless when he saw that he was not greeted by Bruce. The voice said *"I take it you are Ralph?"* replied "Z" with his two Zorba goons standing next to him. Ralph could not believe that he was actually facing a Martian. Before this encounter, Ralph only thought the Martians were a vivid imagination on Mr. High Pocket's part. Once again "Z" asked Ralph the same question but this time attached the needed voice-meter as well as have his goons point their ray guns at his private parts.

Before Ralph could give the Zorba commander an answer, Tom returned to the office and said to Ralph *"Ready when you are."* Instead of Ralph greeting him, the two goons immediately raised their right arm and shouted *"Hail Zorba."* "Z" disgustingly told his men *"Not him you morons, me."* Tom stood in his tracks frozen from what he saw. "Z" then added *"He is the other traitor, remember?"* The larger of the goons said *"Oh Yeah, sorry about that boss."* Ralph overcame his fear and said to the commander *"I see you are the one responsible for our canines disappearing."* "Z" told Ralph that it was part of his master plan. He then pulled out a photo of Mr. High Pockets and said *"I want him."* after handing the photo to Ralph. The Zorba commander then explained to Ralph and Tom that they would make an exchange; Mr. High Pockets for the safe return of their families as well as the rest of the kidnapped canines. He then said *"Give us this Mr. High Pockets and we will give you back your precious ones. Once we are on Zorba, we will send back your canines."* Ralph and Tom had little choice but to go along with what "Z" had proposed. "Z" wrote a ransom note and handed it to Tom. He then said *"Deliver this to your Mr. High Pockets. Tell him to meet us at the park at midnight. And no funny business or your friend here gets it."* Tom ran out of the store as fast as he could and headed straight to City Hall.

Back on Zorba, Zeke was about to give up when the door to his cell opened. He was greeted by one of the Zorba guards. The guard handed Zeke a meal of green beans and green salad and said *"Enjoy it. This is your last meal."* Zeke looked at the food and made a sarcastic human comment. He said *"What. I don't get fries with this order?"* Even Zorba guards don't have a sense of humor. When the guard turned his back, Zeke took the plate of food and clobbered the guard, knocking him unconscious. Zeke grabbed the keys and locked the guard in the cell. He left the cell saying *"Maybe next time you will give me my fries."* The Alien's wife greeted him at the door when he got home and asked *"What took you so long? Long line at the Zorba store?"* Out of breath, Zeke did his best to explain to his wife why he was late. Once he finished his story, Zeke asked his wife where her keys were to her spaceship. She asked him why and Zeke replied with *"I have to go to Earth and save the canines."* Zeke kissed his wife goodbye and took off in his wife's spaceship. She said to herself *"Why can't he donate to Zorba charities like everyone else."*

At City Hall, Mr. High Pockets was busy preparing for a press conference regarding the disappearance of the canines. His secretary buzzed him on the intercom and told the "Yapper" that he had a visitor. When he looked at his appointment book, the "Yapper" saw that he was not scheduled to see anyone until the next day. He asked his secretary who the visitor was and she replied *"He says his name is Tom."* Mr. High Pockets jumped to his feet and greeted Tom with *"Hey pal, what are you doing here?"* and then added *"Did you hear about the canine shortage?"* Suddenly, Zeke shouted *"It's me."* and removed his disguise. Zeke shook his pals paw and quickly told him of the evil plot the Zorba commander was involved in. Mr. High Pockets said *"Well, that explains the canine shortage."* and then asked his Alien friend if he had a plan that would get them back. While they were thinking of a plan, Mr. High Pockets excused himself to go potty and told his friend that he thinks better when on a break.

When Mr. High Pockets returned he saw that Zeke had suddenly vanished. Another knock on the door startled the "Yapper" as he said to himself *"Who could it be now."* Mr. High Pockets opened the door and saw Tom. The "Yapper" said *"Okay Zeke. Enough of the disappearing act. You can take off that disguise now."* He then grabbed the face part of the disguise and tugged as hard as he could. Tom shouted *"Hey that hurts. What did you do that for?"* The "Yapper" said that he thought he was Zeke still in disguise. Tom said *"Do I look like an Alien to you?"* Suddenly, Zeke appeared from behind the curtain. Once again it startled the "Yapper" as he said to Zeke *"Dude, you have to quit doing that to me."* Once Mr. High Pockets regained his composure, Tom handed Mr. High Pockets the ransom note and told the Mayor that the Martians had kidnapped Ralph and their families in exchange for him. Tom then asked Mr. High Pockets *"Do you have a plan?"* The "Yapper" replied *"No, but Zeke does."* Since Zeke had the idea to keep the canines from being destroyed, he gave his friends a drink. Tom liked the green drink and asked Zeke what he called it. The Alien replied *"We call it Zorba juice."* and added *"I got the recipe from Cindy."* After a few more drinks of the Zorba juice, they headed to the park and waited for "Z" to arrive.

It seemed to Ralph that there was no way an Alien could get away with kidnapping canines. He said to "Z" *"You will never get away with this."* "Z" immediately talked about future plans on how he plans on taking over Earth once the canines are destroyed. He then said *"Once I destroy the canines, I will build Zorba stores all over the planet. I will be revered."* Ralph shook his head and said *"Aren't you getting ahead of yourself."* The Zorba commander asked Ralph why he said that and Ralph responded *"Because this story has not gone to print yet."* "Z" said *"I see your point."* and then fired his ray gun at Ralph, instantly disintegrating the clothes Ralph was wearing. "Z" then said *"Let that be a lesson to you. Don't mess with a Zorba."* One of the goons looked at his Zorba watch and told their fearless leader it was time to head to the park. As they left the novelty store, "Z" turned to Ralph and said "*I hope your partner got the message to that "Yapper", or else.*"

Tom, Zeke and Mr. High Pockets arrived at the park early enough to get a vantage point on where the exchange would be taking place. They hid in the bushes patiently waiting for "Z" to arrive with Ralph. Mr. High Pockets looked at Zeke and said "*I hope your plan works.*" Without smiling, the Alien replied "*So do I.*" Within moments, the group saw a light flash at the other end of the duck pond. Tom said to his posse "*That's' the signal, let's go.*" The trio dusted themselves off and side-by-side headed to the center of the park; their rendezvous point. Slowly the trio made their way with music in the background as if they were in a western movie. Tom said to Mr. High Pockets "*Where is that music coming from?*" Mr. High Pockets smiled and said "*Oh, I had a technician install a play box. Kind of adds realism don't you think?*"

Tom said "*There is as far as we go for now.*" as the trio reached their designated spot. Across the pond, Tom could see the shadowy figures of "Z" and his goons and said "*Looks like we are not alone.*" Under the cover of darkness, "Z" maneuvered his way toward the trio. Ralph was behind him with two ray guns pointing at his private parts. One of the goons said to Ralph "*Go ahead; give me an excuse to use this.*" Ralph took a long gulp as he hoped that Tom had figured a way to save him and the rest of the canines. At this point, "Z" gave the command for his men to stop. It was a spot far enough away from the would-be rescuers so that their guns would be useless but theirs were well within range. Smiling, "Z" gave the nod to Mr. High Pockets. The "Yapper" nodded in return and slowly walked toward the Zorba commander. When they were within arms-reach, the Zorba commander said to Mr. High Pockets *"Do you have to play that stupid music? It's giving me a headache."* The "Yapper" said *"Oh, sorry about that."* and gave the signal to shut off the music.

There they stood armed with their choice of weapons and both dressed as if they were in a classic shoot-out. "Z" was the first to say *"So, you are the famous Yapper. I have been waiting a long time for this moment. You have cost me a lot of Zorba votes in the last election."* Mr. High Pockets said *"It's not my fault you don't have a sense of humor."* The Zorba commander told the "Yapper" that on his planet having a sense of humor is against the law, punishable by death. He was quick to add *"I can't wait to see the expression on your face when you face the Zorba squad."* Mr. High Pockets said *"If you want me, you need to let my friends go as well as the canines you kidnapped."* "Z" agreed and told the "Yapper" *"I will release your friends now and then release the canines once you are on board my spaceship and we are safely on our way."* He then added *"As a kind Zorba gesture, I will give you two Zorba minutes to say goodbye to your friends."* Mr. High Pockets asked the commander how many Earth minutes that was and he replied *"You have 30 seconds."*

Mr. High Pockets turned toward his pals and gave them each a hug. He told them that this was for the best in that the needs of the many outweigh the needs of few.

Seems that Mr. High Pockets definitely had watched too many science fiction movies. With tears in their eyes, the "Yapper" walked toward the Zorba commander and said *"Okay, I am ready now."* He walked past Ralph and in passing said to Mr. High Pockets *"I will never forget what you are doing for us."* The rest of Ralph's family joined him as everyone was teary-eyed. They huddled like most people or canines would when they fear that the worst was about to happen. Trying to lighten the mood, Tom sarcastically said *"Looks like we will need a new Mayor."* The gang waved at Mr. High Pockets as he bravely entered the Alien spaceship, never to be heard from again.

Suddenly, the Alien spaceship took off. The canines stayed behind to pay tribute to a fallen comrade. Mr. High Pockets will be remembered for the hero that he was. As the group was paying their final respects to the "Yapper", a familiar voice was heard from behind the group. The entire group turned their heads when the same familiar voice said to the gang *"So, what is all the commotion about? How come I wasn't invited to the party?"* Everyone's mouths were wide open when they saw their beloved "Yapper" had escaped from the goon squad. Ralph hugged his old friend and said *"How did you escape from the Aliens?"* Mr. High Pockets smiled and told his friends that he didn't and that it was all part of Zeke's plan. He placed his paws on Ralph and said *"Let's go home. I will tell you all about it on the way."*

About half-way to planet Zorba, the Zorba commander told the "Yapper" *"We are near the planet Zorba. Do you have any last-minute requests before you meet your demise?"* Mr. High Pockets sat on the floor motionless and speechless. "Z" said to the "Yapper" *"This is your last chance. Say something."* and prodded Mr. High Pockets with his ray gun. Suddenly, the body of Mr. High Pockets started to smoke and soon the Zorba commander saw several springs jut out of the prisoner's body. He said *"What the......."*and reached down to grab his prisoner. "Z" grabbed the collar of Mr. High Pockets and noticed a tag from behind the collar. He read the tag and said *"I can believe this happens to canines but not to Martians.* The tag stated that it was a Mr. High Pockets novelty. A mechanical canine from their own Zorba novelty store; Zorbas R Us. Zeke purchased the novelty while on his way to Earth.

When Cynthia stood after she finished narrating her story, the ladies also stood and gave her a round of applause for having narrated a great story. Cynthia smiled and bowed to the Judges. Once she received her much-deserved accolades, she turned her smile to an evil glare and immediately looked at Rick. She then grabbed the "Rick" bat and slowly walked in his direction. After she took a stance in front of Rick, Marty shouted *"Now Cynthia, be nice. You know it was an accident."* By now Rick was terrified and placed his hands in front of him to protect himself from Cynthia. Cynthia raised the bat and said to Marty *"Oh, I know it was an accident."* When the men heard the comment, they relaxed and sat back down. Cynthia smiled at Rick and shouted Mr. High Pocket's famous command *"Flame On."* She removed the disguise from the bat so that everyone could see that she was holding a ray gun. Without hesitation, she shot Rick. Instead of a ball of fire or streams of strawberry jam, Cynthia shot Rick and froze him in his tracks.

Stunned was not what I would exactly say were the expressions the men gave when they saw their friend sitting motionless in his chair with his arms in front of him and his mouth wide open. Cynthia then held the ray gun in front of her and pointed it to the rest of the men. She then instructed the men to move Rick to a platform located on the other side of the duck pond. Once the men gently placed their friend on the spot Cynthia had marked, they returned to their seats fearful that Cynthia would do the same thing to them. Cynthia joined the rest of the ladies and after she received her high-fives for a well-done prank, she shouted *"Score one for the ladies."*

When the Duck caretakers saw that the prank was over, they exited the Duck pond and stood near the statue. The oldest Duck said *"Well, at least it beats having a scarecrow in the park."* After he smiled, the youngest Duck replied *"Do you think we should charge an admission fee?"* while pointing to the birds flying overhead. The oldest Duck said *"No, maybe he will thaw out by book 12."*

KEEPING A STANDING TRADITION

Adam looked at me and said *"I think it's time for a break."* Considering the pranks that had been played I told Adam that was a great idea, for two reasons. One, to keep the contest from getting out of hand. More importantly, the second reason was my curiosity. I wanted to see first-hand exactly what Cynthia did to Rick. After I told the gang that we were taking a break, I motioned for the men to follow me. The four of us stood next to Rick amazed at the statuesque appearance. Marty jokingly said *"Is he dead?"* I looked at Marty and said *"Of course not."* Harry Sr. waved his hand in front of Rick's face and saw that Rick did not move his head nor bat an eye. He then said to the gang *"Are you sure?"* Harry said *"Well, we need to do something quick."* as he pointed to the birds flying over our heads, circling as if trying to find a spot to land. I told my trusted comrades that I would fix the problem. After I retrieved the ray gun from Cynthia, I moved the selector switch and pointed the gun at Rick. I shouted Mr. High Pocket's famous command and fired a blast at Rick. When we saw that Rick moved, I said to myself *"I can't believe it actually worked."*

Rick said *"What happened?"* as he found himself near the pond wondering how he got there. We took Rick back to his seat and told him that we would explain everything later. I went back to the Judge's table to inform the contestants that we were ready for the next story. Before I could make that announcement, Harry Sr. approached the table and said to me *"Hey, I need you to do me a favor."* I smiled at Harry Sr. and said *"Really. I take it you no longer think that I am a nut job?"* Harry Sr. also smiled and said *"Oh no. I still think that you are a nut job."* and then placed a story on the table. He said that he had been working on the story for quite some time and wanted to know if I could squeeze it in. I looked at the Judge's to see if they were in agreement. Adam said *"Why not? What else can go wrong?"* Beth thought that it would be a nice change of pace and also agreed. So, I announced to the contestants that we would resume the title-quest after I narrated the story given to us by Harry Sr. According to Harry Sr., this was his unique version of "Keeping a Standing Tradition".

Friday mornings were always reserved for me. This was the time I chose to get away from the pranks, the bantering and from Sophie's constant whining on why I won't let her win the lottery. I went to the coffee shop eager to get away from it all. As usual, I sat in a corner booth. When I placed my lap-top on the table, I noticed two waitresses were standing at the counter giggling as if they had heard a joke. It seemed that one of the waitresses smiled when I sat down. She grabbed a cup of coffee and headed in my direction. I smiled at the young waitress and said *"Thank you."* The waitress said *"You must be the Author. I recognize your photo on the wall."* Smiling back at the waitress I told her I was the Author. She then handed me a copy of my last book and asked if I could autograph it for her. When I handed the book to the waitress, she said thank you and then added *"Good Luck."* I was a little startled by the comment she made so I asked the waitress why she made that comment. The young waitress looked at me with an astonished look and said *"Oh no. I take it you haven't heard the news."* She then placed the morning newspaper on the table and returned to her duties.

I put on my reading glasses and read the front page story. It was captioned "Park in Peril". I said to myself *"What park?"* As I read the story, my smile that once greeted the young waitress vanished into thin air. The story talked about a park in our community that was earmarked for demolition to make way for a department store. It further discussed how the store would benefit the economy of the community as well as create new jobs. When I saw the photo of the park, I said to myself *"This can't be."* It was a photo of our park. I continued to read the story on the next page and became more outraged at what I read and saw. On the second page was another photo of the park. This one showed a man and a woman shaking hands while both were wearing hard hats. I glared at the woman in the photo and said to myself *"Why that little hussy."* It was

Annie. Furious was not the only emotion I wanted to show Annie. I quickly called all of the adult characters and told them to meet me at Cindy's house in one hour.

On the ride over to Cindy's house, all I could think about was our beautiful park and of the fond memories we had. It was a place where Ralph had his first litter. The park was first chosen to host our famous reunion. It was a place where the characters could use to perform their unending pranks. Even Sophie had a special date with Jack at the very same park. The children enjoyed the park when they were involved in their title-quest. Our chosen place had been a standing tradition from the beginning. Now we were faced with losing the one place that everyone loved. I did my level best to control my anger before I arrived at Cindy's house. This was one time I was not about to let Annie steal a standing tradition.

Everyone was seated at the round table when I walked into Cindy's house. Without a smile, I placed the newspaper on the table for everyone to read. Cindy saw the expression on my face and said "*Uh oh, that's not good.*" Before I could explain the mood I was in, Harry Sr. said "*Did you bring lasagna?*" I looked at Harry Sr. and replied "*Not now.*" I pointed to the newspaper and told Cindy to read the front-page story. As she read the story, I explained to the rest of the gang what was in the news article. Their looks told me I was not the only one angry about the story. Cindy tried her best to calm me down when she said "*Sorry Hon, but that's how life is sometimes.*" I told Cindy that she might want to reconsider her comment after she read page two. She saw the photo and shouted out the exact same comment I had made earlier to myself at the coffee shop. She said "*Why that little hussy.*" The rest of the group huddled around Cindy to take a peak of the photo. After Marty saw the photo, he said to me "*So, what can we do about it?*" I was just about to tell Marty what I was going to do when I received a text message from Ralph. He said that he had a serious problem at the store and needed my presence. I said to myself "*If it rains, it pours.*" Until I returned, I told the gang to see if they could come up with any information about the so-called developer that Annie was involved with.

For Ralph's sake, whatever problem he had better be more important than what I had found out about Annie and our current problem. I walked into the store and found the Duck care-takers of the pond sitting at Ralph's desk. Ralph asked me to have a seat and then handed me a list. I asked Ralph what it was and he said that it was petition signed by the animals that lived at the park. One of the Ducks said to me "*Hey dude. I thought we had a deal.*" Ralph asked me what kind of deal he was talking about. I told my publisher I would fill him in on the deal after we take care of our current problem. Prior to the title-quest, I hired the Ducks to look after the park and clean up any messes left by the canines. In exchange, they would get recognition in the books along with a possible story-line in the next book. Ralph then said "*I take it you know why they are here?*" while pointing to the Ducks. As soon as I told Ralph that I was at Cindy's house briefing the adults about the problem when he called, Ralph placed a newspaper on the table. He said *"This just came out."* It was a special edition of the morning newspaper. Once again, the front page was filled with news about our park. This time the story announced the ground-breaking ceremony that would start the very next morning. It also included another photo of Annie smiling and posing with a shovel in her hand. When Ralph asked me what I was going to do about it, my cell-phone vibrated. I read a message from Annie. It said *"Meet me at the park at noon."* I hesitated at first but told Ralph I would get back with him after I spoke with the adults. It was time for me to confront Annie.

My mind was a total blank. I wasn't quite sure why Annie requested a meeting but I was curious to find out why our famous park was going to be demolished. There she stood, right at the entrance to the park near the sign the adult characters had built. I looked at Annie and said *"So, what's this all about."* She grinned at me and said sarcastically *"Gee, it's good to see you too."* Annie grabbed me by the arm and suggested that we take a stroll around the park. I mentioned to Annie that I was in no mood for a romantic walk. The co-leader of the Cat Mafia assured me it was not her intention. When we arrived at the gazebo, Annie said *"You see those bulldozers over there?"* I looked but quickly turned my attention back to Annie when she added *"You can prevent all of this from happening."* Before I could ask her why, Annie pulled out a contract from her purse and handed it to me. Again, before I could ask why, Annie handed me another paper. It was a list of demands.

I sat down on the steps to the gazebo and quickly scanned through the papers she handed me. I looked at Annie and said *"You have got to be joking. Have you been out in the sun too long?"* She was quick to say that she suggested I take my time in reading the contract.

Annie took a deep breath and began to discuss the consequences on what would happen if I didn't give in to her demands. She said *"If this park is destroyed, you will not have a place to call home let alone pull your pranks. When that happens, you will lose your story-line. In other words, you and your so-called pet characters will be out of business for good."* It finally dawned on me what the meeting was all about. Since Annie's plots against us have been foiled in the past, this was the only way she could win; through bribery. She knew that I would do almost anything for our characters as well as our way of life. Without the park we would definitely be out of business. For the time being, all I could do was stare at the pond. To break the silence, Annie said *"Tell you what. I will give you until tonight to make up your mind."* She handed me her business card and told me to be at her house later that evening with the signed contract. Before Annie left the park, she once again mentioned the outcome if I didn't deliver the signed contract that evening.

"How could this be happening?" I said to myself as I placed my hands over my eyes. I read the contract and the list of demands for the second time. The contract would give Annie 51% ownership of the "No Sense of Humor" series as well as the novelty business. It would require me to

place the ownership of the shop in her name, which meant
that Ralph and company surely would be out of a job. I am
sure Annie had their replacements already picked out. In
addition, the list of demands was a conditional part of the
contract. It read as follows:

1. Beth would be terminated as the writing assistant.
2. Canines would no longer be involved with the
   story-line.
3. Permanent disbanding of the Canine Mafia.
4. Female adult characters can only narrate stories
   upon written approval from Annie.
5. All male characters will be deleted from the series.
6. Annie will be the new self-appointed writing
   assistant.

It took me a while to muster enough strength to leave
the park. I had no clue as to what I was going to do. No
matter what I did, it seemed that Annie found a way to
destroy our dreams and our livelihood. The worst was yet
to come. I had to break the news to the adults.

Marty must have heard my car pull in the driveway.
He greeted me at the door before I had a chance to knock.
He said *"It's about time you got back. So, what was so urgent
with Ralph?"* I told my old friend that he had the same
problem we had. When he gave me a startled look and
looked at his watch, Marty wondered why it took me so
long to get back considering I was gone for almost two
hours. I told the gang that I had to make a slight detour to

the park. Cindy asked me why so I said *"To meet Annie."* Silence filled the room as everyone could hear a pin drop. Brenda broke the silence and said *"Oh, you went to the park to talk some sense into her, right?"* I replied *"Well, not exactly."* and with a deep breath I added *"I have a date with her later tonight."* All the woman rose from their seats and simultaneously shouted *"You have a what?"* The men backed away from me as they saw the ladies grab several bats. I raised my arms in the air and told the ladies to listen to what I had to say before using the bats.

Once the ladies lowered their bats, I sat down at the round table. Marty handed me a much needed drink and whispered to me *"Dude, I hope you have one heck of a story to tell."* I then told the ladies that I met Annie at the park for a reason. She requested my presence to hand me a contract. I placed the contract and the list of demands on the table. After downing the first drink, I then told the gang about Annie's attempt of bribery. The group was shocked when they read the papers. I then said *"Annie gave me until tonight to sign the papers or its goodbye park."* Marty asked me what I was going to do. I told him that either way, we were out of business. Cindy calmly approached me, placed her hands on my shoulder and said *"Whatever you do, we will be here for you."* She then neatly tucked a pen in my shirt pocket. I asked Cindy where she got the pen. She told me that Ralph delivered it after I had left his shop. The pen was a commemorative pen that was used to help promote the rebuilding of the store.

I left Cindy's house still not sure of what I was going to do. It was just like that proverbial saying "Stuck between a rock and a hard place". No matter what I did, Annie would have control. As I approached her door, I said to myself *"Might as well get this over with."* Annie greeted me as if we were on a date. She dressed provocatively for the occasion. Her apartment was dimly lit and I heard soft jazz in the background. I looked at Annie and said *"Nice try."* She poured me a drink and asked me if I had come to a decision yet. I told the young blond that I wanted to go over the list of demands first before I signed the contract. When she poured herself a drink, Annie replied *"You are not exactly in a position to give demands."* I then told Annie it was either that or I walk away. She took a seat on the sofa and said *"Okay, I am listening."* I placed the contract and the list of demands on the table and said *"I want Ralph and Tom to stay on as my publishers."* Annie said *"You mean our publishers."* After giving her a faint smile I nodded my head in agreement. Annie agreed to my terms. She signed her part of the contract, handed me a pen and said *"Okay, your turn."* I waved her gesture off and used the pen that Cindy gave me to sign the contract. Annie's eyes widened with joy as she placed the contract in her safe. I grabbed my jacket and headed toward the door. Annie said *"You know you can stay for dinner now that we are partners."* I replied *"No thanks. I just lost my appetite."*

Another deep breath was what I needed when I arrived at Cindy's house. The gang had been patiently waiting for me to return with the bad news. Not long after I sat down, we received a surprise visit from Ralph and Tom. I said to the duo *"What brings you two here."* Ralph immediately reached in my pocket and pulled out the pen Cindy had given me. I asked Ralph why he took my pen and he muttered *"You will see."* He handed the pen to Tom. Tom set his lap-top on the round table, unscrewed the pen and plugged it into the side port of his lap-top. After he made a few adjustments, Tom said *"Ready when you are."* Ralph told me that he had a hunch that I was going to see Annie. He had Jack install a receiving device in the pen so that he could record my conversation with Annie. Ralph looked at me and said *"Never trust a hussy."* He also told us that he was able to record the conversation Annie had with another person while she was in the bathroom. I looked at Ralph and said *"We were alone."* Ralph cleared his throat and said *"She was on the phone with Amy."* We all stood around the table and intently listed to Annie's conversation.

Annie was heard telling Amy that she was proud of her latest plan. She told Amy that once she gained control of the company that she would make arrangements to bring her back into the country. Amy was heard asking Annie *"Now that we have control of the company, are you going to keep the park?"* Annie replied *"Are you nuts. I am going to demolish the park first thing in the morning. Those Morons will never know what hit them."* *"Oh, got to go. I have the Author in the other room sweating like a pig. Call you later."* Tom shut off the device and said *"Now what are we going to do?"* I turned to look at everyone and smiled as I took another sip of my drink. Marty also smiled when he said

"*I see that light switch got turned on in your brain.*" He was right. I just came up with a plan. Looking at Ralph, I said "*Muster the canines. We have work to do before tomorrow morning.*" Ralph jumped for joy and said to me "*Way to go Big-dog.*" Tom, still unsure about those eloquent phrases said to Ralph "*How does he look like a Big-dog? He doesn't have four legs.*"

It didn't take long for the canines to arrive at the shop. After I briefed the canines of my plan, I handed each of them a list. I figured that the only way to prevent Annie from destroying the park was to sabotage the equipment. The canines knew time was of the essence as we only had till day-break to complete our mission. I picked up Marty at day-break and headed straight to the park once I received a call from Ralph telling me that our mission was complete. We arrived at the park in time to see Annie get out of her car. When she saw us standing next to the park sign, she said "*I didn't expect to see you here.*" I replied "*I thought that you would leave the park alone if I signed that contract.*" Her evil grin told me the answer I was looking for. She then said "*This will be the new site of the Cat Mafia. Ironic don't you think.*" She then added "*Besides, those Ducks were getting on my nerves.*" Marty and I both grinned at each other when Annie made that comment. She looked at us and said "*What's so funny.*" after placing her hands on her hips. I looked at Annie and said "*Oh, You'll see.*"

Marty instantly raised his right hand and twirled his arm, giving the signal to start our operation. The engines of the bulldozers revved drowning out any comments

Annie had made. Soon, two of the bulldozers headed in our direction. As one of the bulldozers neared Annie's car, I tapped Marty on the shoulder and said *"Watch this."* The operator of the bulldozer raised the blade high in the air and dropped it onto Annie's car, turning it into a matchbox. By now, all Annie could do was watch the show. Her mouth was wide open. She even made the attempt to speak but the shock of seeing her brand-new car being crushed was too much for her to bear. Another signal by Marty to the operators of the bulldozers gave us a glimpse of the second part of our operation. Suddenly, one of the bulldozers neared a van that was close to the pond. The van was the official vehicle of the Cat Mafia. A second shock set in for Annie when she saw the bulldozer push the van into the Duck pond. Soon the bulldozers filed single-file and left the park.

Seeing that Annie was still in a state of shock, I placed my arm on her shoulders and said *"Seems that you need transportation."* I then reached behind the tree and placed her new transportation in front of her. It was a red tricycle, complete with a basket and horn. I then added a sarcastic comment and said *"I would have gotten you insurance but I ran out of time."* Angrily, Annie got on her new mode of transportation and shouted *"This is not the end of it. I still own most of the company. See you in court pal."* As she rode out of the park, I smiled but realized that Annie was right. Marty said *"You do realize that she is going to make your life miserable."* I told Marty that I knew what Annie was capable of doing but at least I had the satisfaction of knowing that our beloved park was safe from destruction.

Later, when I went home to check on Sophie, I received a knock on the door. Sure enough, it was a process server. He handed me papers which showed that I had a court date with Annie on Monday.

On the way to the courthouse, Marty and I discussed all of the possibilities that Annie had at her disposal to end our reign as pranksters. At least she didn't eliminate our poker nights but now that she was in control, I am sure it would be just a matter of time before she would put an end to many of our traditions. Marty and I sat in the rear of the courtroom waiting for the inevitable. Annie walked in and gave us a look of revenge. She whispered to me *"As soon as I am done here, tell your pets they have 24 hours to move out, or else."* Annie was now smiling when the Bailiff called the court to order. The Judge had Annie approach the bench and asked her to state her business.

As soon as she was done with her request to the Judge, the Judge looked at Annie and said *"You look familiar. Have you been in my courtroom before?"* Annie told the Judge no but also told the Judge that he had a prior dealing with her twin-sister Amy. The Judge said *"Oh yeah. Now I remember. She was not successful the last time she was here.* Annie replied *"I know but I am smarter than her."* When Annie handed the Judge the contract, he read the fine print and checked the signatures on the pages. He glanced at Annie and said *"Are you sure?"* He then handed the contract to Annie and said *"Looks like you haven't learned either.*

Case dismissed." My signature was nowhere to be found on the contract so the Judge dismissed the case, for lack of evidence. Marty looked at me and said *"Looks like you got your company back."* I looked at my comrade and said *"Yes indeed."* Pulling the pen out of my pocket, the one Cindy gave me, I said to myself *"Well I'll be."* The pen was an exact replica of a pen that was used in a previous story. A novelty pen that contained invisible ink. It seemed that the pen was mightier than the sword.

When I finished narrating the story, Harry Sr. rose from his seat anticipating the same type of applause that the other contestants had received earlier in the day. It took a little prodding from Beth to get the ladies to at least give Harry Sr. a single clap. I went to shake Harry Sr.'s hand and said *"You may be a veteran, but you are still a rookie."*

Now back to the contest.

CAMP PAWS: THE TAKE-OVER

Cindy gave the nod to Bertha. We were greeted by the ever-so-popular sounds of trumpets blaring in the background. It was Cindy's cue to make her way to the Judge's table. To play the part of a "Queen", Cindy adorned a costume right out of medieval times. She slowly made her way past the men while extending her right arm. The men acknowledged her presence by gently kissing the top of her hand, except Harry Sr. When Cindy approached him he said jokingly *"Does that come with lasagna?"* Cindy immediately snubbed her nose in the air and sat in front of the Judges. I said to Cindy *"I see that the Queen of Diamonds has made her appearance."* referring to the part on how Cindy uses Marty's credit card to buy diamond jewelry. She said in response *"I am only acknowledging your presence because of Beth. All you men are beneath me."* and once again snubbed her nose in the air. I looked at Adam and said *"I see where this is going."* Before any more bantering could be exchanged between Cindy and I, Beth

told Cindy *"You may now begin your story."* and flipped
the hour glass. According to Cindy, this was her specially-
created story called "Camp Paws: The Take-Over".

One saying that I am sure has been quoted many times
was "If at first you don't succeed, try, try again". This was
one phrase that the Cat Mafia had adopted as their new
logo. There were many episodes in which the Cat Mafia
met defeat at the hands of the canines. At one point they
came close to victory but no cigar. I will say this. The Cat
Mafia was one organization that did not take their defeats
well. Just as the canines have always found ways to improve
their use of the novelties, the Cat Mafia looked for ways to
even the odds.

One Saturday morning, Annie called a special meeting
with her henchmen to figure out a plot that would put the
canines out of business. She even sent out fliers to other
organizations asking for their help. Over a dozen felines
responded to the ad. The felines that showed up for the
meeting were not exactly what Annie would call "Cream
of the Crop" but at that point, she would take anything
that she could use. When she called the meeting to order,
Annie told the gang of her plight with the canines and
needed suggestions of a plot that would destroy the canines
once and for all. She then added *"Now think. I want revenge
and I want it now."* as she slammed her fist on her desk.
For several hours the felines exchanged ideas. Most of the
suggestions would bring victory for the felines but would
get them little satisfaction. Annie was frustrated. She
poured herself a drink and noticed one of her henchman

was reading the morning newspaper. Annie yelled at the gangster and said *"If you don't come up with an idea then I suggest you read the want ads."* The gangster told the leader that he was reading a story about Camp Paws.

"Give me that." Annie said to the gangster as she grabbed the newspaper. Annie then added *"What is so special about this Camp Paws?"* The gangster told Annie a brief history of the camp and how it was used to help canines with their behavior problems. Still not understanding how important it was to the meeting, Annie read the article. The article mentioned at first the history of the camp and how it was useful for pet owners. It was used as a place where pet owners could take their pets to work out their problems. The main part of the article discussed the closing of the camp because of revenue problems. There was a photo of myself and the Director of Camp Paws shaking hands as we had discussed forming a fundraiser to seek donations that would save the camp from closing. One of the henchman asked Annie *"Do we still need a place for our new smuggling operation?"* Annie's eyes lit up like the fourth of July and said *"That's it. I got it. The perfect plan."* She told her henchmen to gather around her desk. She then said *"If you can't beat them, join them."*

All of the henchmen looked at each other as if Annie had taken the Author's Prozac. One of the henchmen shouted *"Are you nuts?"* Annie shook her head and told the gang of her perfect plan. The first part of her plan was to foil the canine's attempt to raise the money to save the camp. Then, Annie would buy the camp and take-over the camp for use as their new headquarters. Once the Cat Mafia took over the camp, they would change the name of the camp and use it for cats only. Canines would no longer have a place to go to. She would have the funds diverted to a special account and use the money to buy the camp. *"Brilliant, just brilliant I might add."* Annie said as she tossed the newspaper in the trash. She then gave instructions to two of her henchmen to foil the canine's fundraiser. Annie changed into a business outfit and one of the henchmen asked her where she was going. She replied *"To meet with the Director of the camp."*

Annie arrived at the camp disgusted with its looks. She even commented to her henchmen that accompanied her that the first thing she was going to do when she took over the camp was to remove those dreadful posters of Mr. High Pockets. She said *"Yuk, I hate canines."* They pulled up at the Director's office and went over their script. Annie was going to portray herself as a woman who had a canine that desperately needed help with a problem. She had her henchmen disguise himself as a canine. After Annie introduced herself to the Director, he asked her what he could do for her. Once she explained the problem her canine had, he said *"Sorry miss, but we are not taking any more clients."* Annie pretended that she didn't know the reason why and asked the Director. He told Annie that because of revenue problems, he had to let most of the staff go and he would be closing the gates in less than two weeks unless Ralph and company could save them.

Smiling, the co-leader of the Cat Mafia said to the Director *"What would you say if I was in a position to help you out?"* Before the Director answered Annie's question, Annie pulled out a piece of paper from her purse, wrote a number on it and handed it to the Director. She then said *"Would that take care of your problems?"* The Director's eyes widened when he saw the number. He told Annie *"That would definitely take care of our problems and then some. That is one heck of a donation."* Annie cleared her throat and told the Director that it was not a donation but a buy-out. The Director paused for a moment and told Annie that he would take her offer under advisement but wanted to see first if Ralph could come through for him. Annie told the Director that she would return in two weeks and wished him the best of luck. As soon as the door was closed, Annie told her henchmen *"What a Moron."* The henchmen asked Annie what their next plan was. She told the henchmen to make sure that the other plan was in full swing. After all, her entire plan rested on the notion that the canines would not be able to get the required donations to save the camp.

Meanwhile, back at Ralph's headquarters, Ralph had started the campaign to save Camp Paws. Fliers were placed all over town depicting the plight of the camp and how the camp needed money to keep its gates open. A hotline was created so that people and canines could make contributions. Bruce was placed in charge to keep a ledger as well as answer the numerous calls that would be created from the fliers. For the first week, it seemed that their campaign was working. Near the end of the campaign with only one day left, Ralph wanted to check on the progress of the campaign and see how much money they had raised. He called Bruce into his office and asked him for the ledger. Bruce said *"I don't know why you want to see the ledger."* Ralph gave Bruce a startled look when Bruce added *"There have been no calls or donations for the past week."* It was strange to see that suddenly the donations stopped after the first part of the campaign showed a lot of money was being pledged. Ralph said to himself *"I wonder if people are broke."* He looked at his watch and realized that it was closing time for the store. Ralph had hoped that his crew drew in enough money to save the camp. The next day was the day that the camp was scheduled to shut down.

As Ralph was about to lock up the store, Tom arrived and told Ralph that the canines had a problem. He placed a flier on the table that he found posted throughout town. Tom told his partner *"Seems that someone replaced our fliers with ones of their own."* The flier Tom brought in was of one that displayed the words "Camp Feline". It had a picture of cats that looked as if they were hungry and included a phone number where people could donate to save the cats. Ralph looked at the flier and said *"Well, that explains why our donations abruptly stopped."* He then said to his pal *"I smell a rat."* Tom, still having a hard time with certain phrases said to Ralph *"Don't tell me we need another exterminator."* Ralph told Tom no as he was referring to the Cat Mafia as the ones who replaced the fliers. To confirm his suspicions, Ralph contacted Samantha to see if she could look into the matter. He then called the Director of Camp Paws and gave him the bad news.

Early the next morning at sunup, Annie met with the Director of Camp Paws once again. She saw that the Director was busy packing up his belongings and knew that her henchmen had come through for her. Annie said to the Director *"I take it Ralph couldn't help?"* The Director nodded his head and continued to pack when Annie said *"You know, my offer is still on the table."* He gave her a faint smile and told her that he was still undecided about the offer. She then told the Director *"Maybe this will help in making up your mind."* Annie handed the Director another paper, this time doubling the initial offer. He said *"Wow, this is an offer that's hard to refuse."* The Director took a deep breath and walked toward the window. He saw his staff carrying boxes to their cars. What once was a thriving mess hall was now but an empty building that was padlocked with a sign that read "Closed". All of the posters had been removed, even the ones that banned Mr. High Pockets. When the Director saw the looks that the canines had on their faces, it was too much to bear. He turned to Annie and said *"Deal."*

The Director may have signed the contract but wondered if he was doing the right thing. He handed the contract to Annie and with a huge smile, she handed him a check. Like in any contract deal, the seller said to Annie *"Congratulations. You are now the proud owner of Camp Paws."* The new owner placed the contract in her purse and then said to the Director *"Oh, you must mean Camp Feline."*

The Director rose to his feet and angrily said to Annie "*You said that you would leave the name of the camp alone.*" Annie replied "*Oops. I lied.*" and then spent several minutes telling the Director of all the marvelous changes she was going to make. She then added "*Oh, I have one change I need to make now. You're fired.*" Annie signaled for her henchmen to surround the Director. With another smile she added "*By the way, you are sitting in my chair.*" The new owner of Camp Paws instructed her henchmen to escort the Director off her property. Annie took her position at the desk as the new owner. She said to herself "*I can't wait to tell Amy the good news.*"

Annie plopped her feet on her new desk thinking of how successful her plan was. She was gleaming with pride as well as the satisfaction that the canines would be gone from the camp. Just as the henchmen were about to escort the Director out the door, the front door crashed open and suddenly Annie and her henchmen were surrounded by federal agents. A familiar voice said "*Freeze. You are all under arrest.*" The lead agent instructed her men to surround Annie. While two of the agents held the henchmen at bay, the other handcuffed the new Director. Annie turned beet-red and said to the agent "*What am I under arrest for?*" Before the agent told Annie the reason, she removed her disguise. It was Samantha. Annie once again glowed with that fiery look and shouted "*You.*" Samantha replied "*For starters, how about fraud.*" She then placed one of the Cat Mafia posters on her desk and told the new owner that they found out the Cat Mafia had acquired money through an illicit and phony cause. Samantha then added while she smiled *"Sounds like fraud to me."* Two of the agents then escorted Annie to the front door. Annie turned to look at Samantha and said *"I will be out in six months. And I still own Camp Paws, I mean Feline."*

Samantha faced Annie and said *"I don't think so."* She pulled out a paper and showed it to Annie. It was a copy of the Cat Mafia's bank statement. Circled in red was the number of the check Annie had given to the Director as payment for the camp. What made Samantha smile was what had been highlighted on the statement. It was the words "Insufficient Funds". Samantha the told Annie *"You see, no money, no contract, no Camp Paws."* She then handed the contract to the old Director. Samantha watched Annie's face as the Director tore up the contract. To put the finishing touches on her capture, Samantha reached into Annie's purse and grabbed her cell-phone. Outraged, Annie said *"What do you think you are doing?"* Samantha told Annie that she had one of the agents add a program to the Cat Mafia's account that automatically transferred the money from the account to the Camp Paws account whenever there was a deposit, hence the reason why the check did not clear the account. She then said to Annie as she looked for Amy's phone number *"I wonder what Amy would say when I tell her how gracious you were in saving Camp Paws. You know you should get a medal for that once you are out of prison."* The lead agent then told her comrades to escort Annie to an awaiting van.

As the Director took his position back, he thanked Samantha for saving the camp. She said to the Director *"Don't thank me, thank him."* and pointed to the door as Mr. High Pockets walked in. The "Yapper" greeted the Director by saying *"Hey boss, how's tricks."* Giving Mr. High Pockets a stern look the Director said *"I should have known it was you."* Before the bantering got out of control, Mr. High Pockets asked the Director *"This makes us even, right?"* The Director said with a startled voice *"Even. You still owe me for two mess halls."* The "Yapper" was quick to respond *"Two. But I didn't burn down the second one."* By now, the Director knew he had the last word when he said *"It was your flame-thrower."*

Cindy made a majestic bow in an attempt to get as many accolades as the story-tellers before her once she finished her story. When she returned to her seat, Cindy smiled and said to herself *"Yep, the Queen has returned."* For several minutes Cindy sat patiently without as much as a hint of what kind of prank she was going to perform. Still smiling from her latest performance, she looked at her watch and began a countdown. Cindy flashed the zero sign with her hand and as if he was on cue, Marty rose from his seat and headed to one of the outhouses. I said to myself *"He picked one heck of a time to go to the bathroom."* As you know, we had been involved with the title-quest for several hours. The temperature outside was so hot that even the pets were looking at taking a swim in the Duck pond. I could only imagine what the temperature was like inside one of those outhouses. About 10 minutes had passed and

Marty was still inside the outhouse. I glanced at Cindy and once again she was looking at her watch giving another countdown with her fingers.

When Cindy displayed the zero sign with her fingers, she rose from her seat and headed to the outhouse Marty was in. She gently closed the outside latch of the outhouse and placed a box on the ground at the door. It was the "Man in the Box". Cindy returned to her seat and said to the ladies *"Watch this."* Suddenly, the outhouse Marty was in began to shake as if Marty was trying to leave. He made a few attempts to escape and then shouted *"Hey, someone let me out of here. The door is jammed."* Everyone started laughing when the "Man in the Box" answered Marty *"Let me out. Let me out."* Marty of course answered back and shouted *"Is that you Rick? You better not be playing a joke."* Once again the "Man in the Box" gave Marty a reply. It was hard to control ourselves as their conversation lasted for several more minutes. When Cindy realized that her husband had enough, she unlatched the door to the outhouse. Cindy noticed that her husband had been sweating and said *"You poor dear. Here, let me wipe you off."*

Marty's beloved wife spent several minutes wiping off her husband's face and neck from the towels that she had found in the outhouse. Actually, they were the towels Cindy placed in the outhouse earlier in the day. I am sure you know by now that the towels were a gift from Marty's dad. She then said to her husband *"There. All nice and dry. Do you feel better dear?"* Marty smiled, thanked his wife and returned to his seat. Just as he sat down, Ralph and

Tom saw what was on Marty's face and broke out in a hysterical laughter. It got to a point that Tom laughed so hard that he fell off his chair. Marty shouted out to Tom *"What's so funny fur ball?"* Harry, looking straight ahead to keep his composure handed Marty a mirror. Marty looked in the mirror and found that his face and neck displayed an array of colors that one would find in a rainbow. He said to himself *"What the......"* Marty turned to look at his wife as if he was going to get an explanation. Cindy shouted *"The next time I wear one of your ties, you better not be asking for cheesecake."*

CANINE SCAVENGERS: BATTLE OF THE SEXES

Beth adored our next contestant. According to Beth, there was something about Bertha that made her very likable. I was always under the impression it was because she had a sense of humor and that she was one lady who did not take any crap from the men. The ladies loved her personality. Especially Cindy. Cindy enjoyed Bertha's company as she knew Bertha was a strong ally. When Bertha handed me the story that she was going to narrate, I smiled as I saw that Bertha selected one of my favorite topics; Battle of the Sexes. Competition between men and women can be fun but at times could become quite fierce. I am sure you remember when Marty challenged the ladies to a contest in setting up a campsite. Even card games between men and women can be extremely competitive. For Bertha's story, let's just say that a battle between the sexes took on a different meaning when she decided to write about the competitive nature of our canines. According to Bertha, this is her story of "Canine Scavengers: Battle of the Sexes".

It had been an exhausting week for Ralph and Tom. They had been swamped with novelty orders all week. Penny and Mary Ann also had their paws full while working at the pet store. Business may have been flourishing but the canines needed a break. Ralph and Tom wanted to treat the ladies to a special night. The duo wanted to take their wives to a fancy canine diner and afterwards find a romantic place where they can dance the night away. Mary Ann and Penny thought that it would be a good gesture on behalf of the men. Or, as Mary Ann would put it *"It's about time our husbands got with the program."* Romance as you know was not one of Ralph's strongest traits. To him, romance was having fun in the hot-tub with Mary Ann and then gorge himself on beans and wieners. Tom was quite the opposite. He felt that keeping the spark alive in his relationship with Penny would certainly gain him a lot of benefits. Mary Ann had hoped that Ralph could learn a thing or two from Tom. At least in her eyes, one night of romance was better than none.

Ralph and Tom selected the best diner in town. To add to the aura of romance, the ladies convinced their husbands to have the night on one of their poker nights. It would show the ladies how true their husband's intentions were. At this point, Ralph and Tom knew better than to disagree with their wives. Tom even managed to get Pixy and Dixy to babysit the litter for an evening. The foursome soon embarked on their romantic voyage. Their dinner was superb according to Mary Ann. The couples held hands while they indulged in romantic conversation. After dinner, the husbands took their ladies dancing. Ralph found a dance club that was perfect for his kind of dancing. The couples were seen dancing the night away on a romantic walkway adorned with flowers. It was a night that the ladies will always remember. Since the ladies had their treat, Mary Ann and Penny told their beloved husbands that they would have their treat when they got home. That is, provided that the children were asleep and Pixy and Dixy didn't eat them out of house and home.

The men were in luck. When the couples arrived home, their litter was fast asleep. Mary Ann paid Pixy and Dixy once she checked the kitchen to make sure there was still food in the house. When Pixy and Dixy left, Ralph whispered to Tom *"Time to have our fun now."* My publisher told the wives that they will be in the hot-tub waiting for them. Mary Ann looked at Penny and said *"Gee, it's nice to see that our husbands think of only one thing."* Penny returned a sarcastic comment and said *"Yeah, food."* Sure enough, when the ladies joined their husbands, they saw the husbands gorging on their favorite snack. Mary Ann hoped that the outfits she and Penny wore would deter the husbands away from their snack.

Once the husbands saw the outfits the ladies were wearing, they became enamored with more thoughts of romance than their snacks. After a while, the foursome were enjoying the solitude and the romantic perks. Mary Ann asked Ralph *"Why can't you be more like Tom?"* Ralph asked his wife what she meant. Mary Ann told her how

Tom always found ways to do something for Penny in a romantic way. Ralph blurted out to his wife *"This is not a competition you know."* Soon Ralph changed the subject away from him by telling the gang *"At least we are not as competitive as the adult characters."* Ralph then went on to mention the ways the adult characters compete against each other. He even mentioned Marty's latest quest. Ralph smiled at Tom and then said to his wife *"Besides, we wouldn't want to be competitive against you two. It wouldn't be fair, you know, with you being women and all."* Mary Ann stood up to wipe herself off and said to Ralph *"Really."* Penny added *"It sounds like a challenge to me."* Tom added his mix to the competitive nature and told the ladies *"How about this. You two come up with a challenge by breakfast."* The ladies agreed and then left the hot-tub. Ralph looked at Mary Ann and said *"Hey. Where are you two going? I thought we were going to have some more fun?"* Mary Ann replied *"To work on our challenge."*

The next morning Ralph and Tom went to the kitchen eager to start their day with a great breakfast. At first they forgot about the challenge especially considering how much canine juice they consumed the night before. Penny saw the husbands enter the kitchen looking as if they were run through a washing machine. She said to Ralph *"You look like crap."* Mary Ann poured the husbands coffee to wake them up. After all, she had a lot to discuss with the famous duo. Once the kids were off to school, the ladies joined the men at the table to discuss the challenge. Ralph looked at Mary Ann and said *"So, you two really want to go through with it?"* When the ladies nodded in agreement, Ralph then said *"Okay, but I hope you two are gracious losers."* Penny took that comment as an opportunity for a wager. She said to the men *"Care to place a wager on that?"* Ralph and Tom smiled at each other knowing that no matter what the ladies would wager, they would come out as the winners. Ralph looked at Penny and said *"Okay, let's haggle."*

After the haggling had stopped, which by the way only lasted a few minutes, the couples agreed to a great incentive to be given to the winners of the challenge. The losing team would cook dinner for the winning team for one week in meals of their choosing. In addition, the winning team would have their photo displayed at the novelty store. Tom looked at Penny and said *"What's the challenge?"* Penny glanced at Mary Ann and then told her husband *"It's a surprise. Besides, according to you two, you guys are going to win anyways."* The men agreed and were then told that the challenge would commence at daybreak the next morning in the park. As the men were leaving the house, Ralph whispered to his partner *"This is going to be a piece of cake. I think our first night we should have steak."*

What can I say? A classic battle of the sexes with bragging rights on the line. Ralph and Tom were eager to show the ladies their superiority. The ladies knew they had the upper-hand. After all, they were the ones who came up with the challenge. At the break of dawn the next morning, the couples headed to the park. Ralph and Tom spent most of the ride to the park trash talking the ladies in an attempt to throw them off their game. Mary Ann said to herself "*They have no clue to what they got themselves into.*" The day prior to the challenge, Mary Ann and Penny spent the entire day at the park setting up the course for their challenge. When they arrived at the park with their husbands, they explained the rules of the challenge. Mary Ann told the husbands that each team would be required to go through five stations. At each station, the team had to find a piece of a puzzle. A table was set up near the end of the course for each team to assemble their puzzles. Once the team assembled their puzzles, they would run to a bell located near the park sign and ring the bell. The first team to correctly assemble the puzzle and ring the bell would be declared the winners.

To make the contest more interesting, Mary Ann told the husbands that she hired a special Judge to oversee the challenge. When Penny saw that the husband's faces had turned a flush color, she said "*You two are not afraid are you?*" Ralph told Penny that it didn't matter who they hired because his team would win the challenge. Mary Ann looked at her husband and said "*I am glad you feel that way sweetie.*" Ralph's beloved wife turned her head and said "*She is here now.*" Standing over the canines and for obvious reasons creating a large shadow was Nurse Bertha. She smiled at the ladies and said "*Are these the patients, I mean victims.*" while pointing to Ralph and Tom. Mary Ann told Bertha that she was there to observe the challenge. Bertha misunderstood because she thought it would be a challenge to examine the duo. Mary Ann then smiled at Bertha and said "*Maybe next time.*"

Before the canines embark on their challenge, let's take a look at the unique stations that Mary Ann and Penny set up for the contest.

First, two lanes were set up side-by-side that contained the stations. Each team would start at the same time as Bertha would start the event by blowing a horn. At the first station there are three beehives on a table. All three look identical except for their contents. One was filled with exploding red dye, one was an actual beehive and the other was filled with candy as they all contained a piece of the puzzle. Each team could only select one beehive and they hoped that they would select the right one. For the next station there would be three "Man in the Boxes" set up on a table. All the boxes would have a piece of the puzzle. These boxes were also modified for the challenge. Cranks were installed on the side of the box so that it resembled that popular "Jack in the Box". The canines would be required to select only one box and turn the crank. One box contained candy, one box contained exploding dye and the other box contained a pop-up figure.

Station three was a new station created by Penny. For this station, each team would be required to climb a ladder and ride a slide into a sandbox. Inside the sandbox were exploding mines that were buried. There was only one mine that was classified as a "Dud" that contained the piece of the puzzle. It didn't matter how many mines the canines found as long as they found the puzzle piece. Each mine contained different exploding dye packs and probes would be used to locate the mines. Station four was a modification of the famous slide-for-life that was used in previous stories. Here, there would be three mechanical canines that stood on a platform that looked identical. A puzzle piece would be attached to the tail of each mechanical canine. Instead of the water slide, a catapult was built under the platform. The canines had one chance to select the right mechanical canine as the other two would catapult them into the Duck pond.

Last but certainly not least was a newly created station made by Mary Ann. She decided to use this station last to test the husband's agility skills. A plank was laid out over a vat full of maple syrup. Each team would be required to walk the plank blindfolded. A puzzle piece was attached to the end of the plank. What was unique about this station was that Mary Ann installed a sensor under the board. If anyone were to step on the button that activated the sensor, the board would tilt sideways sending the person or canine into the vat of maple syrup. This was one station that both canines had to complete to get the puzzle piece, regardless of the amount of attempts it took. If a canine fell in the vat, he or she would have to start over.

Finally there is the puzzle. The puzzle, once assembled, would recite a phrase. Each team is required to write down the phrase on a piece of paper and bring it with them when they reach the finish line. Again, the first team that rings the bell wins the challenge. Bertha went over the rules with the teams once she placed them on the ready line. She whispered to Ralph *"Do you know what happens to men when they beat their ladies?"* Before he could answer,

Bertha added *"They have to answer to me."* Our beloved nurse smiled at Ralph and Tom and then gently donned her latex gloves. Bertha then said to the duo *"I will see you two at the finish line."* Knowing that Bertha had just put the scare into their husbands, the ladies asked the men if they wanted to back out of the contest. Ralph held his head high in the air and said *"No Way."* Bertha grabbed the horn and positioned herself between the teams. She raised her hand in the air and gave the command to start the challenge.

Mary Ann and Penny ran to station one and knew which beehive to select. They chose the center beehive. Penny poked the beehive and instantly candy flushed out of the beehive. Mary Ann reached into the beehive, grabbed the puzzle piece and said to Penny *"Got it. Let's go."* The ladies turned to look at their husbands as they headed for the next station. Ralph and Tom arrived at their first station not as eager as the ladies. When Ralph saw three identical beehives, he looked at Tom and said *"Which one do we choose?"* Tom couldn't decide which beehive to choose. Ralph said to Tom *"Hurry up and pick one. The ladies are getting away."* Tom closed his eyes and chose the center beehive. When Ralph jabbed the beehive, a mist of exploding dye greeted the pair in the face. Once they wiped off their faces, Ralph grabbed the puzzle piece. While on their way to the next station, Tom said to Ralph *"At least we didn't pick the one with the bees inside."*

By now, the ladies had already reached station two. They chose the "Man in the Box" on the left. After cranking the box, they removed their next puzzle piece that was attached to a pop-up figure. Penny shouted to her partner "*On to the next station.*" Tom and Ralph had sprinted to station two in an attempt to catch up with the ladies. It was Ralph's turn to choose the novelty. He crossed his fingers and chose the center box. Tom cranked the handle and as soon as the box popped open, Tom squinted his eyes as if he was expecting another exploding dye packet. Luckily Ralph chose the pop-up figure. Ralph grabbed the puzzle piece and told his partner to follow him to the next station. Smiling, Tom said to Ralph "*Right behind you partner.*"

Each team reached the next station at approximately the same time. Mary Ann and Penny went through station three with ease. Together they slid into the sandbox and safely stood in a spot avoiding the exploding mines. Penny grabbed her probe and found the mine marked "Dud". She grabbed the puzzle piece and the ladies tip-toed out of the sandbox to avoid the rest of the mines. They ran a swiftly as they could to the next station. When the ladies arrived at station four, Mary Ann looked back to see where Ralph and Tom were. The duo was standing at station three reading the sign. Ralph looked at Tom and asked "*So, what do we do here?*" Tom told his partner that they ride the slide into the sandbox and grab the puzzle piece. Ralph told his partner "*Sounds easy. I'll go first.*" Ralph slid down the slide and said to himself "*Wow. This is fun.*" He landed butt first in the sandbox and after he realized that he sat on an exploding mine, he said to himself "*Oh crap.*" His butt looked like an orange beach-ball. Tom stood on the top of the slide and yelled to Ralph *"Oh, I forgot to tell you. Watch out for exploding mines."* Ralph looked up at his partner and said *"Now you tell me. Get down here."*

Tom slid down the slide and yelled *"Wee."* He landed in a safe spot and as cats normally do, Tom landed on his feet. Ralph told his partner *"Show-off."* and instructed Tom to grab a probe. Tom took a step toward Ralph and heard a clicking sound underneath his left paw. Realizing that he had just stepped on an exploding mine, he yelled to his partner *"Uh oh."* Before Ralph could tell his partner not to move, Tom raised his left paw. The mine exploded as Tom now had a reminder of station three. His left paw was the same color as Ralph's butt. They searched the rest of the sandbox for the mine marked "Dud". As soon as they found the puzzle piece, Ralph and Tom headed to the next station. Mary Ann and Penny saw the men approach their station and quickly began their task to uncover the next puzzle piece.

The slide-for-life had been one of the favorite stations used by the children as well as the adults. Mary Ann liked this new version as the men had no clue as to what awaited them. The men only remembered the water slide. Penny and Mary Ann picked the center canine. They grabbed the puzzle piece from the mechanical canine's tail and immediately ran to the next station. Meanwhile, Ralph and Tom stood at the exit to the sandbox exhausted. Somehow, they mustered enough energy to run to the next station. Ralph said to Tom *"Remember, this is the water slide. I don't want to take a bath."* Tom looked at the mechanical canines and said to his partner *"I think we should pick that one."* Ralph tugged on the canine's tail and pulled the puzzle piece. Suddenly, the ground shook beneath Tom and Ralph as the duo clung to each other like glue. Their worst fear came true when a catapult sent the men into the Duck pond. Even though the pair emerged from the pond soaking wet, they thought that the ride was fun. Ralph said to Tom *"At least I held on to the puzzle piece."*

Mary Ann and Penny arrived at station five knowing that they had a comfortable lead over the men. They grabbed their blind-folds and stood in front of the plank. Penny asked Mary Ann if she remembered where she had installed the sensor. Mary Ann told her partner not to worry because their blind-folds were see-thru. Once the ladies were safely on the other side of the plank, Penny grabbed the last puzzle piece and headed to the table. Since the ladies had a remarkable lead on the men, they decided to take a break and set up lawn chairs to watch the men go through the last station. Mary Ann said to Penny *"Might as well have some fun."* Ralph and Tom saw the ladies sitting in their lawn chairs sipping on ice tea. Tom looked at his partner and said *"They like to show off, don't they?"* Since Ralph had gone first on a previous station, Tom took his turn at the lead. He placed the blind-fold over his eyes and with cat-like precision walked across the plank without setting off the sensor. He looked back at his partner and said *"Piece of cake."* Ralph was not about to let his partner out-do him.

Smiling, Ralph yelled out to Tom *"Watch this."* He placed the blindfold over his eyes and began to walk the plank. Tom shouted to his partner *"That's it partner. You are half-way home."* Ralph grinned and gave his partner the thumbs-up. My publisher was about two feet from the end of the plank when he heard a click. Just as he said to himself that he knew he had stepped on the sensor, Tom shouted to his partner *"Quick. Jump."* Ralph leaped as far as he could but didn't reach the far side. He ended up in the vat that was filled with Maple Syrup. Tom grabbed his partner by the paw and pulled him to safety. He sarcastically said to Ralph *"Do we have time to eat some pancakes."* Meanwhile, Mary Ann and Penny saw what Ralph looked like when he emerged from the vat and decided to take a photo. To add to Ralph's embarrassment, Mary Ann turned to Penny and said *"Watch this."* Mary Ann grabbed a remote control device from her bag and pointed it to a tree near Ralph. Suddenly, a bag full of black and white feathers fell on Ralph. To his dismay, Ralph looked like a Penguin.

It didn't take long for Ralph to realize who was behind the prank. As he gave his wife an evil glare, Mary Ann said out loud *"Oh crap."* The ladies put their chairs away when they saw the men head to the table. Mary Ann and Penny reached into their bag to grab the puzzle pieces. They were shocked when they saw that the puzzle pieces had stuck to their paws. Each of the ladies frantically attempted to shake the pieces from their paws but was not successful. It was then that the ladies realized the puzzle pieces were super-glued to their paws. Ralph and Tom smiled when they arrived at their table. It did not take the duo long to assemble the puzzle. Once they wrote the inscription on a piece of paper, Ralph and Tom calmly walked toward the finish line. They paused for a moment to discuss who was going to ring the bell as well as look back at their wives. Just as Mary Ann and Penny finally put their puzzle together, Tom rang the bell declaring their team as the winners. In case you didn't know, the inscription on the ladies puzzle read *"Men Rule."*

As soon as Bertha finished her story, the ladies hovered around her and gave their favorite nurse a hug for such a fine narrated story. The Judges also applauded Bertha. As I sat down I said to myself *"Wait a second. There is something missing."* Suddenly it donned on me what was missing. Bertha was not seen with her latex gloves. Before I could tell the rest of the Judges my observation, the ladies went to stand behind their husbands. Bertha then walked toward the men and as soon as she stood in front of Harry, Bertha pulled out her gloves. I said to myself *"There it is. The missing piece to the puzzle."* Our beloved nurse smiled as she donned her gloves and looked at each of the men. I could see that the men were very uncomfortable as neither of the men knew which one was about to get a prostate exam.

Bertha looked at Harry and said *"I like the way you take care of Daisy Mae. You are safe."* She then slowly took a step and turned to face Rick. Bertha said to him *"Cynthia has already gotten her revenge. You are safe."* Again, Bertha took another step and turned to face Harry Sr. She said with a grin *"Your wife is a great cook. I love her lasagna. You are safe."* Lastly, Bertha took a final step and turned to face Marty. Stretching her gloves to give Marty the impression that he was the one selected for her exam, Bertha said to Marty *"You are married to Cindy. You are not safe."* Bertha then removed a strap from her waist and tied Marty to his chair. The rest of the ladies were shocked when they saw Bertha remove Marty's pants. Our nurse then went to the park flag-pole. She lowered the park flag and replaced it with Marty's pants with glow in the dark letters. After she proudly displayed Marty's pants, the ladies gave her a high-five for a prank performed well and above the line of duty.

Even the Duck caretakers liked their new addition. The eldest Duck waddled his way to Bertha and said *"Nice touch."* As the Duck maneuvered his way back to the pond, one of the other Ducks asked him what all the commotion was about. Once the eldest Duck explained the prank that Bertha pulled on Marty, he said *"Look at it this way. At least we can now find our way home in the dark."*

DINNER AND A MOVIE

Adam looked at me and said *"Do you think we need another break?"* Seeing Marty without any pants on made me believe that a break was needed. I rose from my seat and as soon as I headed toward Marty, the ladies gave me an evil look. Cindy and Bertha were holding bats in their hands, padding them as if they were about to be used. I wisely returned to the Judge's table. I then said to Adam *"Ah. The heck with it. Marty deserved it anyways."* When Adam saw the look that the ladies were giving me, he responded *"Smart move."* Beth then called for our next contestant. Brenda handed the Judges a copy of her story. As she sat down, Brenda gave Harry Sr. a wink. I think it was safe to assume that somehow Harry Sr. would be involved in the next prank. Beth saw the wink and whispered to me *"I can't wait to see what happens when this story is finished."* I flipped the hour glass and told Brenda that she may now start her story. According to Brenda, this is her story called "Dinner and a Movie".

Mary Ann and Ralph were sitting at the kitchen table discussing events that needed to be planned for the week. Two important events that needed to be planned were Ruby's graduation and Tom and Penny's anniversary. Mary Ann went to the calendar that was posted on the wall and circled the dates as a reminder to Ralph. She knew how forgetful her husband can be and didn't want Ralph to forget those important events, especially after he had forgotten their own anniversary. When she realized that there was another important event the following week, Mary Ann asked Ralph *"Sweetie. Your birthday is next week. Would you like to do something special on that day?"* Ralph returned a comment with a grin and said *"Just you and a hot-tub."* Mary Ann knew that her husband wanted that but she wanted to do something special for him. She told Ralph *"I have an idea. Why don't we host a dinner party and celebrate all three events at the same time."* Ralph actually thought that his wife had a great idea.

Before he left for work, Ralph told his wife that she could plan anything she wanted. His beloved wife told him that she would fill him in on her plans when he got home that evening. As soon as Ralph went to work, Mary Ann and Penny worked on the invitations to the party. Penny finished writing the last invitation and said to Mary Ann *"Does Ralph know how lucky he is? I can't believe you are so forgiving."* Mary Ann's silence and grin led Penny to believe otherwise. She said to Mary Ann *"Wait. I recognize that look. Okay, what gives?"* Mary Ann then told Penny of her plan to get even with Ralph. Mainly because of the fact that the week after Ralph's birthday was her birthday. Mary Ann said to Penny *"If this doesn't teach him a lesson, nothing will."* Together, Penny and Mary Ann worked out the details of their dinner party. The idea came from a previous story in which Cindy had hosted a dinner party for the canines.

For this event, Mary Ann would only invite the adult characters who were married. Unfortunately, Rick and I had to sit this one out. First she would host a lavish dinner and after dinner, Mary Ann would have certain canines perform a skit in the form of a murder mystery. She would have the adult characters attempt to solve the mystery as a team. The canines that Mary Ann solicited for the event included Mr. High Pockets, Pixy and Dixy, Ruby, and Sophie, with Ralph as the main course, I mean murder victim. Instead of ad-libbing the story as shown in previous mysteries, Mary Ann would write specific scripts for each canine. She would have the canines read the scripts in front of the adult characters. Ralph was told of the dinner party when he got home from work. He was happy knowing that his favorite food would be served at the party but was not thrilled with being portrayed as the murder victim. To him, it left open too many possibilities for other canines to pull pranks, at his expense.

Once Penny had sent out the invitations to the party, both her and Mary Ann knew that it was just a matter of time before they would be bombarded with phone calls from the canines. The entire week Mary Ann and Penny spent preparing the costumes for the canines. Tom wanted to know what roles the canines were going to have. Penny told her husband that Mary Ann wanted to keep it a secret until the day of the party. The ladies must have known that Tom was acting as a go-between to find out more information for Ralph. Marty and Cindy looked forward to the event. As far as Cindy was concerned, it was the only time Marty actually considered the event as a date. Harry and Harriett were anxious to see what kind of pranks Mary Ann had in store for Ralph. Harry Sr. wanted food only as he could care less about the mystery. He told Eve *"If you have seen one canine mystery, you have seen them all."* It did give Eve a chance to participate in an event that in previous stories she had taken a seat on the side-lines. Even though I was single, Mary Ann invited me to attend the event to take pictures. Here I am wondering *"What in the world is Mary Ann up to?"*

Mary Ann chose a Friday evening to host the event so everyone had to fore-go their usual, traditional night of fun. She set up a lavish buffet table for her guests. Once the characters had their fill of food, Mary Ann instructed the adults to take their places in the living room. She set up a row of chairs to give the impression that the adults had first-class seats. My chair was behind the row of chairs. When the adults took their seats, Mary Ann instructed the canines to put on their costumes while she explained to the adults the roles that the characters were about to play. She also handed the adults a list of the items in the house that could be used as the murder weapon. They were the rope, a container of lipstick, a black tie, and a lead pipe.

The host thanked her guests for attending the party. She then took out her cue cards and told the adults the type of characters that were involved in the murder mystery and who was selected to act out their roles. Ralph would portray an evil Banker named Mr. Moneybags who would do anything to get rich at anyone's expense. He would ultimately end up as the murder victim. Sophie would act out the role of a jilted lover. Since Sophie and Ralph were involved in a relationship in previous stories, Mary Ann chose Sophie's character name to be Miss Jezebel. Ruby would star as an innocent little girl named Miss Cupcake who went to visit the evil banker to persuade him to not foreclose on her parent's farm. Mr. High Pocket's would make his popular appearance as a former partner of the evil banker who was swindled out of a land purchase. Mary Ann fittingly chose his character name as Mr. Yapper. Pixy and Dixy were chosen to play the part of two employees who had been fired by the evil banker for not collecting money from certain businesses that were owned by the banker. They were known by their nick names; the "Dough Boys".

Penny was given the cue to dim the lights to start the event. Ralph entered the living room and took his spot on center-stage. Mary Ann then introduced the first scene to her guests.

Scene One: Mr. Moneybags and Miss Jezebel

Miss Jezebel wanted to surprise her boyfriend with lunch. When she arrived at Mr. Moneybag's office, she noticed that the door to his office was slightly open. Miss Jezebel could hear that her boyfriend was on the phone. She first thought that he was on the phone with a client so she decided to wait a moment until he was done. While Miss Jezebel was waiting, she overheard her boyfriend say *"You are the one for me babe."* Miss Jezebel said to herself *"Why that two-timer. Wait till I get my hands on him."* She then burst into her boyfriend's office. Startled, Mr. Moneybags said nervously *"Babe, what a nice surprise."* Miss Jezebel replied *"Oh don't babe me. I heard you on the phone."* He then told her that he had been secretly seeing another woman. Shocked beyond belief, Miss Jezebel Placed one hand on her head as if she was going to faint. She looked at the crowd and then said *"I will see to it that you never do that again."* Miss Jezebel looked around the office to see if there was anything that she could use to hit her boyfriend. She grabbed the lamp from Mr. Moneybag's desk and held it high in the air. Just as she was about to hit her lover, Miss Jezebel shouted *"You are not worth the effort."* She placed the lamp on the desk, slapped Mr. Moneybags in the face and stormed out of the office.

Mary Ann stood in front of the adults and clapped signaling that the scene was over. Ralph and Sophie stood next to her so that they could get recognized for their performance. Once Sophie took a seat and Ralph returned to his spot on the stage, Mary Ann introduced the characters for the next scene.

Scene Two: Mr. Moneybags and Miss Cupcake

Mr. Moneybags was busy at his desk signing foreclosure notices when his secretary announced that he had a visitor. Miss Cupcake walked in the office clad in a cowgirl outfit as if she had just competed in a rodeo. The evil banker asked the young lady *"What can I do for you young lady?"* Without smiling, Miss Cupcake told the banker who she was. She then asked the banker if there was any way that he could change his mind about foreclosing on her parent's farm. Mr. Moneybags said *"No way. By this time tomorrow I will sell the farm and be rich."* Mr. Moneybags immediately broke out in an uncontrollable evil laughter. It was all that Miss Cupcake could take. She grabbed her rope and with a twirling motion lassoed the evil banker to the ground. Miss Cupcake then opened the window in his office and began to pull the evil banker toward the window as if she was going to hang him. When she heard a knock on the door, Miss Cupcake regained her composure and untied the banker. She whispered to him *"This is not over. I will be back."* Miss Cupcake grabbed her rope and left the office.

Everyone applauded Ruby's performance. We could tell that she was definitely Daddy's little girl. When she joined

Sophie, Mary Ann sighed as if she was ever so proud of her daughter. She then introduced the characters for scene three.

Scene Three: Mr. Moneybags and Mr. Yapper

Without so much as a knock, Mr. Yapper barged into his business partner's office outraged over a recent deal. Clad in western gear and sporting those popular six-shooters, Mr. Yapper slammed a deed on the banker's desk and said *"What is the meaning of this?"* He then explained to the banker that the land that was sold to him was to be for his cattle. Instead, Mr. Yapper told his partner that he sold him a deserted parking lot. Grinning, Mr. Moneybags looked at Mr. Yapper and said *"Yep, a sucker born every minute."* Furious, Mr. Yapper said *"You will not get away with this."* He turned to face the door as if he was leaving. Mr. Yapper saw a lead pipe lying on the floor near a chair. Mr. Yapper grabbed the pipe and held it high in the air as he approached the banker. Suddenly, the banker shouted *"Wait. I will give you your money back."* Mr. Yapper tossed the lead pipe in the corner. He then drew his six-shooters and pointed them at Mr. Moneybags. He told the banker *"I will be back in one hour. You better have my money, or else."* Mr. Yapper smiled at the audience, gave a quick tug on his moustache and left the office.

When the scene was finished, Mr. High Pockets held his paws high in the air as if he was congratulating himself for giving a star performance. I said to myself *"What a ham."* Mary Ann entered the room also making the same comment to herself. She whispered to the audience *"Next time I will hire a Monkey."* After Mary Ann received an applause for her comment, she then introduced the characters for the final scene.

Scene Four: Mr. Moneybags and the Dough Boys

The evil banker had been waiting patiently for his employees to return to the office with money as well with news about a building purchase. The employees were sent to convince a particular owner to sell the building to the banker. Clad in business suits and wearing black ties, the Dough Boys stood at the banker's door hesitant about entering the office. They did not have good news for their boss. Once they found the nerve to confront their boss, the banker said *"Well, is he going to sell?"* One of the Dough Boys cleared his throat and said to the banker *"No. We were too late."* and added that the owner sold the building to another banker. Mr. Moneybags was furious. He rose from his seat and shouted *"You two are Morons. Chimpanzees can do a better job than you too."* The banker grabbed the cash from the Dough Boys and said to them *"You two Morons are fired. Now get out of my office."* Outraged at being fired, the Dough Boys removed their black ties and approached the banker as if they were going to strangle him. Immediately Mr. Moneybags raised his paws and said *"Now boys, don't do anything that you will regret."* As luck would have it, a knock on the door saved the banker. One of the Dough Boys noticed that there was a box of donuts on the banker's desk. He grabbed the box and the pair headed toward the door. One of the Dough Boys shouted *"You have not seen the last of us."*

Mary Ann stood and applauded Pixy and Dixy for a great performance. She then told the adults that there was going to be a brief intermission so that Ralph could prepare for the murder scene. Once Ralph went to the kitchen, the adults shouted out comments as if they were reading from a script. Actually, Mary Ann handed the adults the script to add to the drama of Ralph's pending demise. Marty shouted *"Let's hang the furry creature."* Harry Sr. cleared his throat and shouted *"No. That's too good for him. Let's boil him in oil."* Finally, Harry made the final comment and said *"I have a better idea. Let's drown him in his own hot-tub."* Meanwhile, Tom was busy putting fake blood on Ralph when they heard the comments. Tom said to his partner *"Gee. They are out for blood, aren't they?"*

Once Ralph returned to the stage, Mary Ann announced to the adults that it was time for them to solve the murder mystery. On cue, Penny turned off the lights. A loud scream echoed throughout the house giving the effect that someone uncovered a dead body. When the lights came back on, Ralph, or Mr. Moneybags, was lying on his desk. Mary Ann told the adults that they were free to examine the body and to find the murder weapon.

Marty and Cindy were the first to examine the body. While Marty looked under the desk, Cindy noticed that Mr. Moneybags had something clenched in his right paw. She told her partner *"Honey, look what I found."* Cindy opened Mr. Moneybags paw and found a tube of red lipstick which happened to be the same color Sophie wore in her scene. She told Marty that tube was probably poisoned since there was a lipstick stain on Mr. Moneybag's right cheek. Marty and Cindy wrote down who they thought the killer was as well as the murder weapon. They concluded that Miss Jezebel killed Mr. Moneybags with poison lipstick.

Meanwhile, Harry and Harriett decided to look for clues in another room to see if they could uncover a murder weapon. When Harriett found a black tie hidden near the hot-tub, she said to her husband *"I have an idea. Follow me."* They went to the crime scene to examine the body. Under Mr. Moneybags head lay another black tie. This one was attached to the back of his collar. Harry looked at his wife and said *"Guess we know who did it."* Harriett immediately wrote down their results. Unlike Marty and Cindy's conclusion, the pair wrote that the Dough Boys committed the murder and used the black ties to strangle him. Satisfied that they found the right culprits, they joined Marty and Cindy.

Eve grabbed Harry Sr. by the hand and led him to the kitchen. Harry Sr. smiled and said *"Good idea. I am hungry."* Once Eve slapped her husband on the arm, she told Harry Sr. to look for the murder weapon. Harry Sr.

looked under the kitchen table and saw something that was sticking out of a box. He said to Eve *"What's in here."* The pair uncovered a rope. Eve gave her husband a startled look and said *"You don't think that innocent little girl did it?"* Before Harry Sr. could answer, Eve took her husband to the crime scene. When they saw that there was a deed to a farmhouse tucked under the body, Harry Sr. and Eve realized who killed Mr. Moneybags. Eve wrote down in her book that Miss Cupcake was the killer and that she strangled the evil banker with the rope. They in turn also joined the rest of the adults since they claimed that they solved the mystery.

Before the adults could get the chance to inform Mary Ann of their findings, the lights dimmed twice as the adults then saw an eerie glow emanate from the desk where Mr. Moneybags lay. Suddenly, a body emerged from the darkness wearing a black robe. The face at first could not be seen as it was covered by a hood. This person slowly approached the victim with a large pair of scissors. Everyone gave a shocked cry as the person removed the black robe. A familiar voice said *"I have you where I want you."* It was Nurse Bertha. Instead on donning her latex gloves, she raised the scissors high enough above the victim so that the adults could get a great view of what she was about to do. Nurse Bertha then said to the victim *"It is time to remove your private parts."* With an evil laugh that made everyone's hair stand straight up, Bertha slowly worked the scissors and stood over the body.

Ralph woke up in a cold sweet. He leaned over to Mary Ann and said *"Honey. Wake up."* She asked her husband why he woke her up from a sound sleep. Ralph told his wife that he was about to have his private parts cut off by Nurse Bertha. He then told her the story about how he was involved in a murder mystery and then everyone wanted him dead. Mary Ann looked at her husband and said *"No one is out to get you. You just had a bad dream. Now go back to sleep."* Ralph wiped the sweat from his fore-head and said to his wife *"Maybe you're right but it sure seemed real."* Ralph also said to his wife *"I promise I will never forget an important date."* He kissed his wife and rolled over to get some sleep. Mary Ann smiled and said to herself *"I certainly hope so."* Tucked away under her side of the bed was a nurse's uniform and a pair of scissors.

Brenda received a standing ovation for her narrated story. The ladies loved the thrilling mystery and gave Brenda several hugs of approval. When she sat down, Brenda looked at Harry Sr. and gave him a wink. On cue, Harry Sr. winked back and removed a remote control device from his shirt. Prior to the start of the story, Brenda set a mechanical bird in a tree that was situated behind the ladies seats. It was her turn to pull a prank on Marty. Harry Sr. was about to activate the remote when suddenly the men's attention turned toward the volleyball court. As Brenda had just finished narrating her story, several woman clad only in bikini's strode toward the court. This couldn't have been a more perfect time for Harry Sr. to strike. While the men were busy watching the young beauties,

Harry Sr. activated the remote. A large mechanical bird emerged from the tree. Harry Sr. maneuvered the bird towards Marty, its intended target.

Harry Sr. said to himself *"I got you now."* For some reason Harry Sr. hit the wrong button. Instead of hitting a release button that was supposed to release fake dog-poop on Marty's head, Harry Sr. activated another maneuver button. The mechanical bird then flew over the ladies. Suddenly and without warning, the mechanical bird released its package on an unsuspecting victim; Nurse Bertha. Shocked and outraged was not the look the Judges saw that came from Bertha when we saw the fake dog-poop had been dropped in Bertha's lap. The rest of the ladies desperately tried to calm Bertha down. Harry Sr. saw the fiasco and said to himself *"Oh crap."* He then reached into a bag and removed a pair of pants. Once Harry Sr. placed the device in the back pocket, he tapped Marty on the shoulder and said *"Hey pal. I feel sorry for you."* and handed Marty the pants.

Marty said to Harry Sr. *"Thanks pal."* While he tried to give his attention to the ladies on the court, Marty put on the pants and once again thanked Harry Sr. As he turned to face the ladies on the court, he saw something fall out of his back pocket. He reached down, grabbed the device and said to himself *"What's this?"* Suddenly his wife shouted *"Marty. How could you do this to Bertha?"* Marty looked at his wife and saw that the ladies were giving him an evil look. When he saw that Bertha rose from her seat and started to run in his direction, Marty said to himself *"Oh crap."* and tossed the remote on the ground. Marty then ran as fast as he could to avoid being captured by Bertha. He was only able to find a safe haven at an outhouse. Marty locked the door and hoped that it would be enough to keep Bertha away. Just when we thought that the prank was finished, the Duck care-taker and his girlfriend approached the outhouse and placed an "Out of Order" sign on the door. The male Duck looked at his watch and said to his girlfriend *"Looks like it's quitting time. Want to grab dinner and a movie?"* The female Duck replied *"Might as well. Looks like Marty will be in there for a while."*

VACATION DAY
FOR A MARTIAN

I knocked on the door to the outhouse and said *"Marty. You can come out now. It's safe."* Marty was hesitant at first because he felt that it was just a ploy to have someone else pull a prank on him. I once again told Marty that he was safe and that Brenda told Bertha her idea of a prank. My comrade unlatched the door and slowly peeked his head out of the outhouse. I said to Marty *"See."* and pointed to Bertha. When he was satisfied that Bertha was not going to get him, Marty rejoined the rest of the men. I returned to the Judge's table and told Adam that we were set to announce the final contestant. If I would have known that Marty was the target of many pranks, I would have renamed the event "Get Marty Day". It would have been easier to have Marty sit center stage in front of the Judges table and have the ladies line up to take turns at a prank.

When Anna approached the Judge's table her smile toward me led me to believe that she overheard my comment to Adam. She asked the Judge's if it was against the contest rules to perform a prank first instead of after narrating the story. The Judge's looked at each other and said *"Why not."* Anna thanked the Judges and headed toward the men. She grabbed Rick by the hand and escorted him behind a tree. A few moments later Rick emerged with his head completely shaven. Of course everyone applauded Anna as they thought that shaving Rick's head was her prank. By all means Anna was not quite finished. She then grabbed Harry by the hand and escorted him behind the tree. Just like Rick, Harry emerged with is head shaven. When Harry sat down, his father said *"You too look like me. Great job."*

Once again, the ladies applauded Anna for her prank. However, Anna was still not done with her prank. She stood in front of Marty while holding a pair of sheers. Patiently Anna waited for Marty to agree to have his head shaven as well. After a lot of prodding by the men, Marty said *"Why not."* As Marty rose from his seat, Anna instructed Marty to sit down as she wanted to shave his head in front of the ladies. She then placed a white apron over his shirt and while the ladies stood to take pictures, she shaved Marty's head. After a brief applause by the adults, Anna placed Marty's hair in a plastic bag. She then handed the bag to the Duck care-taker. When the Duck thanked Anna, he headed toward the outhouse Marty had used. Curiosity got to all of us as we followed the Duck to see what he was going to do with Marty's hair. It seemed that the adults were not the only ones interested in embarrassing Marty that day. On the side of the outhouse, we saw that the Duck had drawn a picture of Marty with the caption *"Marty was here."* The Duck care-taker then removed Marty's hair from the bag and glued the hair to the picture, giving the picture a more life-like appearance. He then added more hair to give the impression that Marty had a moustache. When he finished adding the hair, the Duck care-taker said to himself *"There. That should do it."* Marty said *"Very funny Mr. Duck."* The Duck care-taker turned to face the adults and he saw that the ladies were smiling at the picture. He said to the ladies *"Hey. Can't a Duck have a sense of humor?"*

Now was the time that the ladies applauded Anna for a well-done prank. We returned to our seats so that Anna could narrate her story. Right before she handed us her copy of the story, she looked at Rick and Harry and gave them a nod. They removed the so-called bald wigs that had been expertly placed on their heads by Anna. Everyone saw that Rick and Harry still had a full head of hair. Marty was stunned to see that he was the only one other than Harry Sr. that was bald. He looked at Rick and Harry and said *"How could you guys do this to me?"* He then gave Anna an evil look and shouted *"I want my hair back."* Beth laughed so hard at Marty's comment that she almost knocked over the timer. She was able to restrain herself from more laughter and as she flipped the timer, Beth told Anna that she may now start her story. According to Anna, this was her version of "Vacation Day For A Martian".

Zeke had been proud of his accomplishments. He was a loving father to his little Zorbians, has a devoted wife, a new-found friend, and a home befitting a king. The only problem Zeke had was that his job demanded a lot of his time and energy. Every night he would come home exhausted. One Thursday night, Zorba time, Zeke arrived home anxious to spend a relaxing evening with his wife. Zeke's wife knew how demanding her husband's job was and how tired he always was when he got home from work. After dinner, Zeke's wife told her husband *"Dear, you really need to take some time off from work."* Zeke knew that his wife was right but told her that he needed the extra Zorba credits to repair his spaceship from his last encounter on Earth. Zeke's wife then said *"Now that you have your spaceship fixed, why don't you pay a visit to your friends on Earth?"* Zeke told his wife that she had a great idea. When Zeke saw that his wife had a curious look about her, he thought to himself that his wife's idea was strange considering she was against his last visit on Earth. Zeke looked at his wife and said *"I see. I take it you don't have an ulterior motive for me to go to Earth?"*

Before Zeke could ask more questions about how his wife was so eager to let him go to Earth, his wife pulled out a book and placed it on the table. Zeke looked at his wife and said *"What's this?"* Zeke's wife told her husband that she wanted to write a book about his adventures on Earth. She then added *"I call it the Book of Zorba's."* Zeke smiled when he saw the cover of the book. The cover layout showed the famous park that the adults use for their pranks as well as a photo of Mr. High Pockets on the front cover. Zeke's wife said *"My publisher told me that it would be a best seller."* Zeke gave his wife a startled look when he opened the book and saw that the pages were blank. He said to his wife *"But dear, the pages are blank."* That was when Zeke found out his wife's true intentions regarding his trip to Earth. She told her husband *"You can kill two Zorba's at once. Visit your friends and do some research for me for my book."* Zeke's wife then commented on the fact that she had never met a real-life canine and that all she knew about canines was from what she had read in their local Zorba newspaper called "The Zorba Gazette". Even though his wife had an ulterior motive, Zeke agreed to the trip.

Meanwhile, back on planet Earth, Ralph and Tom were conducting their usual meeting on Friday to discuss business. At least that's what they told their wives. Actually, it was a tradition that Ralph started so that the group could get together to discuss what kind of fun they were going to have at their poker night. Mr. High Pockets was also included and gave his secretary the excuse that he would use Fridays to mingle with his voters. Just as the meeting got under way, Mr. High Pockets received a message from Zeke. He informed the "Yapper" that he would be paying him a visit. Mr. High Pockets read the message and said to the gang *"Look who's coming to dinner."* The canines were pleased that they were going to see their friend once again. Ralph asked the "Yapper" when Zeke was supposed to arrive. Mr. High Pockets told Ralph that his message didn't tell him when he would be arriving. Bruce suddenly interrupted the meeting and said to the canines *"Uh guys. You better come see this. There is a little green man answering the canine hotline."* The trio dashed into the other room. Clad in a short-sleeve shirt, sunglasses and sporting an unusual beach hat was Zeke.

Ralph was the first to notice Zeke's appearance and commented to Zeke *"You look like a tourist."* After the usual pleasantries were exchanged, Zeke told his pals the reason for the visit. Zeke asked his pals if he could help him before he returned to his home planet. He also told the canines that if he didn't return to Zorba with the research his wife wanted that she would see to it that he no longer has fun in the hot-tub. Ralph looked at Zeke and said *"I understand that pal."* So, the trio sat down with Zeke and worked out a schedule to aid Zeke in his quest for knowledge. The canines decided to first take Zeke to the local canine library. Afterwards, Ralph would take Zeke on a tour of their beloved town to show his pal how the canines lived. Then, as a bonus, Zeke would get a chance to spend time with pet owners. Since Ralph became Zeke's official tour guide, one could only imagine who those pet owners were going to be.

On the way to the library, Zeke mentioned to Ralph how much he liked riding in the dog-mobile. Ralph snickered when he mentioned how he knew about the trip Mr. High Pockets and Zeke took to visit Daisy Mae. Zeke asked Ralph *"Will we be visiting that bird today? Our annual Zorba game is next week and I have to provide snacks for the game."* Ralph told Zeke that Daisy Mae was well guarded, especially after what had happened the last time Zeke zapped Harriett's prize bird. He then added *"Sorry pal. The bird is off-limits."* When the pair arrived at the library, Zeke saw the sign on the door and said *"We have a building like this on Zorba."* Ralph asked his friend what it was called on his planet. Zeke replied *"The Zorba."* and then added *"It's short for The Zorbian Organization for Runts, Beings and other Animals."*

When Zeke saw the rows of books displayed on the shelves, he was amazed at how many books described canines. Ralph said to his pal *"First, we have to get you a library card."* He took Zeke to the Librarian's desk to get his card. Once the card was printed, Ralph told his pal that all he needed to do was put his paw print on the card to make it valid. Zeke asked Ralph *"What is a paw?"* After Ralph showed the young Alien his right foot, Zeke replied *"I see."* and immediately showed Ralph his four arms. Zeke then asked Ralph *"Which one do I use?"* Ralph told Zeke to pick one. After Zeke made his mark on the card, the Librarian handed the card to Zeke and told him he was able to check out the books that he wanted to read. Ralph and Zeke went through every aisle to find books that would be helpful for his wife's research. My publisher was amazed when he saw Zeke load up a cart full of books. He said to Zeke *"That is an awful lots of books to read."* Zeke told Ralph that it would not take him long to read the books and that he could read the books in less than 240,000 Zorba minutes. Ralph asked his green friend how long that is in Earth minutes. Zeke replied *"One hour."*

After the pair loaded the books in the dog-mobile, Ralph drove Zeke around town. They went from shop to shop while Ralph explained the various businesses within the community. Zeke was thrilled with the tour of the canine community. Just as the pair finished their tour, Ralph received a message from Tom informing him that there were problems with certain orders. Ralph told Zeke that his presence was needed at the shop but he would take him to a pet owner's house first. When Ralph told the Alien that he would be there for a while, Zeke told Ralph that he needed to return to his planet soon since his wife was expecting him. Ralph said to his friend *"Just call your wife and tell her your spaceship broke down. Works for the humans."* After a brief phone call, Ralph drove Zeke to Marty and Cindy's house. Before their arrival, Zeke told Ralph that he hoped that his extended visit would not get him in the Zorba house. Ralph smiled as he knew what Zeke was referring to. He handed Zeke that famous "Get out of the Dog House" free card and said *"Give this to your wife if she gives you the look."*

Marty had just finished working on his proverbial "Honey Do" list from Cindy when Ralph and Zeke arrived. He was glad to see his pal as visits from him were rare since he became a publisher. Marty said to Ralph *"Hey pal. What brings you here?"* Ralph told his former owner that he brought Zeke to the house so that he could learn about canines and their pet owners. Marty looked at Zeke and said *"Oh, I didn't recognize you with that beach hat."* Zeke told Marty that he wanted to blend in with the canines as the reason why he chose that outfit. He then told Marty that his main purpose was to gather research for his wife's book. Marty grinned at Zeke and said *"Oh, so your wife is writing a book too?"* When Marty told Zeke the name of the book, Zeke pulled out his Zorba meter to look up the definition of Morons. Zeke cracked a faint smile and said *"I guess that means your wife is writing about the adult male characters."* Before Zeke and Marty continued with their bantering, Ralph told Marty that he needed to return to the store. Ralph told Zeke to have fun and that he was in good hands.

Cindy emerged from the kitchen thrilled to meet Zeke. She had heard a lot about the little green Alien. Marty told her that Zeke would be spending a couple of days with them to do research on pet owners. Of course Cindy would have to start the bantering session by saying to Zeke *"Too bad your wife is doing research on canines. If she was doing research on Morons, I would let her probe Marty's brain."* Without hesitation, Zeke pulled out his Zorba meter. Marty asked Zeke what he was doing and Zeke replied *"Calling the wife to see if I can bring you home for dinner."* Cindy smiled at Zeke and said *"You have a sense of humor."* Since Zeke was accepted into the pet owner's home, he gave Cindy a gift as a way of saying thank you. Cindy opened the box and was amazed at what she saw. It was a green sphere. She asked Zeke what it was and he replied *"We call it the Zorba ball. If you ask a question to a person who is holding the ball, the ball glows. The person has to tell the truth otherwise a green mist sprays on that person's face."* Cindy thanked Zeke and said to herself *"I can't wait to try this on the men."*

When Marty saw the sphere, he came up with an idea for a prank. He told his wife that he thought it would be a great idea to host a BBQ the next day and introduce Zeke to other pet owners. Marty didn't want to ask his wife outright to invite Elizabeth and her prissy canines to the party as she would know that he was planning something. So Marty used a different approach and made references to who they would invite to the party. It ended up in his favor when Cindy suggested that they invite her mother. Marty said *"Honey. That is a great idea."* Since the group was already on the subject of a BBQ, Cindy asked Zeke what kind of food does he like to eat. Zeke handed a list to Cindy of his favorite snacks. Cindy looked at the list and didn't recognize the items. She asked Zeke *"Where can I buy these snacks?"* Zeke replied *"You can buy them at our local Zorba store."* and handed Cindy a stack of Zorba credits. Cindy smiled and said *"Cute. But I am sure I can find something at our local store."* As Cindy headed out the door, she shouted *"Make sure he behaves."* Marty responded *"Yes dear, I will."* Before the door was closed, Cindy added *"I wasn't talking to you. I was talking to Zeke."*

Talking about food as well as the BBQ made Marty very hungry. He asked Zeke if he knew how to cook. Zeke told the pet owner that he cooks for his wife all the time. He then went to the kitchen to prepare a snack for Marty. When he returned just a few minutes later, he said to Marty *"Try this. This is a known delicacy on Zorba."* Marty ate the dish Zeke made and said *"Wow. This is great. What do you call this?"* Zeke replied *"We call it pancakes."*

Marty thought that the food was so good that he wanted more. He went to the kitchen but froze in his tracks when he saw what Zeke had done to Cindy's kitchen. It was as if a hurricane went through the house. There was food everywhere. Marty said to himself *"Cindy is going to have my goose cooked when she sees this."* He turned to look at Zeke and said *"When Cindy sees what you did to her kitchen, she will definitely want you to take me to Zorba."* Seeing that Marty was going to be in trouble, Zeke said *"Not a problem. Watch this."* The green Alien pulled out his ray gun, flipped the selector switch and fired a wide-ranged spray at the kitchen. Instantly, the kitchen looked spotless, even better than before.

Marty said to himself *"Wow. I have to get me one of those."* while pointing to the ray gun. He asked Zeke if the ray gun had other uses. After Zeke explained to Marty the wondrous uses of the ray gun, Marty said to Zeke *"How would you like to help me pull a prank on my mother-in-law?"* At first Zeke was a little hesitant and asked Marty why he would pull a prank. He then told Marty that on his planet, they don't' pull pranks on their in-laws. Marty asked Zeke what his people do instead and Zeke replied *"Oh, we just move them to another planet."* Marty smiled and sarcastically said *"Maybe later."* It would please Marty to see Elizabeth move to another country but he would definitely end up living out his days in the dog-house if Cindy found out that he was the one responsible. Marty then told his friend of a plan to once again get even with Elizabeth. He showed Zeke a story from one of the "No

Sense of Humor" books and asked Zeke if he could pull a prank on Princess and Queenie like Ralph did in that story. Zeke replied *"What's in it for me?"* Marty said to the Alien *"Oh, you are good."* and then told him that he would give him several novelties to take back with him. Marty also used the excuse that it would help with the research of his wife's book. Once Zeke agreed to the prank, Marty told Zeke *"Remember, not a word to Cindy."*

After dinner that evening, Cindy decided to treat Zeke to a home movie. Actually, she wanted to see Marty's expression when she showed Zeke the film from a prank she had performed on Marty in a previous story. As soon as the group saw Marty's butt glowing in the dark, Cindy asked Zeke *"Do you think your wife could use this in her book?"* The only thing Marty said to himself was *"I can't wait until the BBQ."* Cindy went to bed early because of the work she had to do in preparing for the BBQ. This left Marty and Zeke alone to work out the details of their future prank. Marty went to the closet and pulled out Ralph's old bus-boy uniform. He told Zeke that the outfit was what Ralph had worn when he pulled a prank on Princess and Queenie. Marty also told Zeke that he could keep the uniform. Zeke said to himself *"I wonder how many Zorba credits I will get if I sell this on the Zorba Internet?"* For the rest of the evening, well, let's just say it was the calm before the storm.

The next day, Cindy greeted her mother and Adam at the door anxious to catch up on latest events. She told her mother about their visitor and how much she was looking forward to her mother meeting Zeke. Meanwhile, Marty and Zeke were on the patio preparing the food for the BBQ. Zeke was wearing Ralph's uniform and as in a previous story, he had a beer in one hand and a spatula in the other. Marty heard that Elizabeth had arrived and said to Zeke *"Okay. Remember the plan."* Cindy escorted her mother to the patio and introduced her to Zeke with Elizabeth's prissy canines by her side. After the pleasantries were exchanged, Marty took the ladies to the table and served them drinks. Princess and Queenie stood near Zeke waiting to be acknowledged. Zeke pulled out his script and said to the canines *"Wanna play doctor?"* Princess snubbed her nose in the air while Queenie said *"Not with those things."* referring to Zeke's four of everything. She then added *"Besides, we don't do wanna-be actors and bus-boys."* As the prissy canines went to the back of the yard to chase after their favorite chew toys, Zeke scratched his head as he did not understand the terms the prissy canines used. He pulled out his Zorba meter to look up the terms. When he found a photo of Ralph next to the terms, he said to himself *"Oh, I understand now."*

As soon as Zeke finished cooking the food, Marty gave Zeke the nod to start the prank. Zeke pulled out his ray gun and aimed it at his intended target; Princess and Queenie. Suddenly, the prissy canines rose in the air as if they were a hot-air balloon. Right before Zeke raised the canines in the air, he zapped the canines so that they could not bark. Zeke slowly maneuvered the canines to a tree branch high above the crowd. He placed his ray gun in his holster and said to himself *"Not bad for a wanna-be actor."*

Just as Cindy had finished telling her mother of her idea to write a book, Zeke rang the dinner bell. Marty stood up and said *"Dinner is now served."* He then prepared the ladies a special plate and served them with a grin only Adam could see. Cindy told her mother that Zeke was a fine cook and added *"He even brought with him his own recipe from his home planet, I mean country."* Elizabeth ate the hot-dog and was amazed at how good it tasted. She turned to Zeke and said *"This is amazing. You just have to give me your recipe."* Elizabeth then asked Zeke if she could have more. Zeke returned to the table and gave Elizabeth two more hot-dogs. After she ate the hot-dogs, Elizabeth once again commented on the taste. She looked around the yard and saw that her precious canines were not to be seen. Elizabeth asked Marty *"Where are my precious ones?"* Zeke tapped Elizabeth on the shoulder and handed her Princess and Queenie's dog-tags. He then said to Elizabeth *"Hey toots. What do you think you are eating, Oscar Meyer Wieners?"*

Elizabeth was beyond shock. She shouted *"My precious babies."* and fainted. Marty laughed so hard that he fell of his chair. All Adam could do was shake his head as he said to himself *"Yep, Marty will need a good divorce lawyer."* After he composed himself, Marty helped Cindy revive Elizabeth and gave the nod to Zeke to return the prissy canines. Cindy of course apologized to her mother for Marty's behavior and told her that Marty would pay dearly for the prank. Elizabeth took her precious babies and stormed out of the house with neither one saying a word. After Elizabeth left, Cindy told Marty that he had a lot of explaining to do. She was so mad that she could not be in the same room with her husband. She stormed out of the house and told Marty that his explanation better be good when she returned. This was the cue for Zeke to make his departure. Marty said his goodbye to Zeke and gave him the novelties as promised. Cindy returned home in time to see Zeke take off in his spaceship. She was about to confront Marty about his prank when she received a distressing phone-call from her mother. Seems that Princess and Queenie hadn't spoken a word since they left Cindy's house. Marty realized what the problem was and said to himself *"Oops."* Zeke forgot to reverse the spell. When Marty saw the evil look Cindy was giving him, he immediately sent a text message to Zeke asking him if it was too late for him to come to dinner.

Of course Anna received a standing ovation for her fine narrated story. Adam broke open his bottle of Scotch to toast the ladies for their efforts. Once Adam and I made our selection as to who won the contest, we left the park and congratulated Beth. As I was leaving, I said to Beth *"Too bad I don't have a sense of Humor."* and gave her a huge grin. Beth said to herself *"I wonder what he is up to."*

So, once again it's time to select the winner of the contest. Would Cindy regain her title as Queen? Or do you think that there will be a new champion?

THERAPY AT ITS BEST

Since we are on the subject of title-quests, I decided to include this story for the sake of the men. Actually, little did the men know that the ladies wanted to add to their merriment once their title-quest was over. If there was any one adult character that always and I mean always remembered the pranks pulled by the men was Cindy. She wanted the men to know that despite the outcome of the ladies title-quest that she was still "Queen".

About mid-way through the men's poker night there was a knock on my door. I had been expecting Beth to arrive and give me the sealed results of the ladies title-quest. Instead, standing at my front door clad in a blue uniform was a pizza delivery guy. Luckily for us, Harry Sr. ordered pizza. We thought it was only fair since he devoured Eve's lasagna. The men were thrilled with the fact that they now had ample food that energized their bantering evening. Just as the pizza delivery guy was leaving, Beth and Brenda arrived. Beth said *"I see that you men are having your own party."* Harry Sr. smiled as best he could with a mouthful of pizza and said *"Hey toots, you need to get in on this stuff."* Beth of course declined and told the gang that the ladies were waiting for her to return. I asked Beth if she had the results of the contest. She said *"I will have the results for you on Monday morning."* At this point, the men could care less about the results. Food and bantering were the only things on the men's mind that evening.

Brenda cleared her throat and asked the men if we could do her and Beth a favor. She mentioned that they were doing research for a story in the next book and wanted to know if we could help in that research. Marty was a little skeptical of the request. He was one that certainly knew the ladies were up to something. After all, how often do the women come to the men's poker night asking for a favor? I was just as skeptical as Marty but asked Brenda *"Okay Brenda, what can we do for you?"* While giving us that popular flirtatious smile, Brenda handed a business card to each of the men. Harry Sr. didn't appreciate being interrupted while he was eating and said *"This better be good."* I looked at the business card and asked Brenda what it was all about. She told the men that she and Beth needed us to see a therapist. I looked at her and said *"Are you nuts? Maybe you need to see a therapist."* Brenda quickly explained that the therapy session would be for research purposes only since the pets had their session in a previous book. According to her, it would add a nice twist to a revised story. As soon as Brenda mentioned a twist to a revised story, that proverbial light-bulb flashed above my head. I immediately knew that what she had in store for the men had the words "Cindy Prank" written all over it.

Marty could sense a plot in the making and told the ladies *"No way are we going to see a therapist."* The rest of the men nodded in agreement. Even Harry said no and asked Brenda *"Why don't you have the rest of the ladies help you?"* Beth responded *"The ladies are tired from their title-quest."* and added *"Besides, they said no."* Brenda then said with a determined look *"If you do this for us, we will make it worth your while."* Suddenly, the men stopped eating as their eyes were now focused on Brenda. She said *"We are prepared to offer you your own shot at a bantering title, for one night."* Beth placed a large dish of lasagna on the table for the men. In addition, Brenda handed each of the men a sealed envelope that contained a story. She then placed the hour-glass on the table still in the box along with a remade copy of our famous "Exclusionary Rules". Beth said to the men *"You can have your quest tonight provided you each see the therapist in the morning. The appointment time is on the back of the card."*

Beth and Brenda embraced each other waiting for the men to give them their decision. I looked at the ladies and said *"You know what?"* once again stealing Jolene's famous quote. I added *"I know I can't speak for the men so let's put it to a vote."* I looked at Harry Sr. and he said *"Hey, I have lasagna. I'm in."* Rick on the other hand had not been privy to Marty's previous pranks with the ladies as his curiosity got the better of him. Smiling, he said *"Why not? I'm game."*

Harry agreed when he said *"Might as well since Harriett has me cleaning out the garage in the morning."* Marty paused and placed his hand on his chin. After contemplating a few thoughts from what seemed like eternity, he said to Beth *"I might consider it if we have another incentive."* He then smiled and told the ladies that he would agree only if the winner could have his photo taken and sent in to the local newspaper. Beth and Brenda shouted *"Deal."* as every ones focus was now on what I was about to say. I looked at each of the men. Their looks told me I better agree or else. Even though I was still skeptical, I gave the ladies the nod. Maybe it was just the ladies being nice to the men. Only time would tell. Beth and Brenda once again gave each of us a flirtatious smile and left. Beth whispered to Brenda and said *"I can't wait to tell Cindy. She will be so proud of us."*

As soon as the door was closed, I said to the men *"I hope you guys know what you are doing?"* I was not surprised that the men ignored my comment. All I could see was the men devouring Eve's lasagna. Shaking my head, I went to refill my drink when I suddenly stopped dead in my tracks. When that proverbial light-bulb flashed in front of me I said to myself *"I knew it."* Before I could mention to the men what I knew, Rick was rubbing his hands in anticipation as he was about to open the box that contained the hour glass. I suddenly shouted out to Rick *"Stop! Don't open the box."* I grabbed the box from Rick and placed it out of arms reach on the kitchen counter. Rick gave me a puzzled look and said *"What did you do that for? We need that for the contest."* I grabbed my drink and sat down to explain to the men the reason why I thought the ladies were so nice.

Marty said jokingly to me *"Maybe Brenda is right. You do need to see a therapist."* I placed book three on the table and asked Marty if he remembered the story Cindy narrated for her title-quest. He said *"Oh yeah."* and started on a reminiscent story about the pranks that were played on the ladies that evening. Marty finished with *"Yeah. Those were good times."* After taking a sip of my drink, I asked Marty if his dear wife ever forgave him for those pranks or ever played a prank on him that was just as devious. When he replied *"No."* I opened the book to the story titled "The Therapy Session". Once Marty refreshed his memory, he said out loud *"Well I'll be…."* and then added *"You mean to tell me that we have been set up?"* I shook my head yes and since Harry Sr. was not involved in that quest, I quickly filled him in on the pranks Marty bestowed upon the ladies that famous evening. On that particular ladies night, Marty bought a new hour glass for the ladies to use. It came from his dad's novelty store. The hour glass was designed to explode with red ink when turned over.

Harry Sr. said *"You don't think the ladies would do that to us?"* I was quick to respond *"Obviously you don't know Cindy that well."* and retrieved the box that contained the hour glass. I flipped the box on its side so that the caution sticker was exposed. Sure enough, the box did come from Martin's novelty store. The sticker read *"Caution. Box contains exploding hour glass. Red dye included."* Rick asked *"But what about the other pranks. You have been home all day so I am sure Cindy didn't get a chance to set anything up."* Harry said *"Wait. Didn't Beth use the bathroom before she left?"* Suddenly, the men rose from their seats as we all went to investigate a potential prank in my own bathroom. We noticed that the toilet paper had not been touched so at least we had the satisfaction knowing that our butts were not going to be glowing in the dark that evening. Just as in the previous story, I checked the toilet seat cover. I noticed it was slightly raised and said to the men *"I thought the toilet seat was kind of high."* Pointing to the seat cover, I saw that the famous clacker device had been attached, courtesy of Beth.

After dismantling the device, the men went back to the kitchen to refill their drinks. For a few moments we spent trying to figure out how and why the ladies decided to pull such a prank on us especially after we gave in and gave them another shot at the title. I said to Marty *"I have to hand it to Cindy, she is devious."* Rick soon blurted out *"So, what are we going to do now?"* Smiling, I said *"Let's give the ladies what they want."* Harry Sr. looked at me and said *"Yep. You really need to see a therapist."* I then told the gang that we should let the ladies think that their plan worked but plan one of our own. In keeping with tradition, I asked Rick to deal the cards. Once the cards were dealt, Marty asked me what I had in store for the ladies. When the men folded the cards, I presented my plan that would surely be the envy of the men. Harry said *"Okay Mr. Author. Let's see if you have a sense of humor."*

My plan was simple even though that getting the upper-hand on Cindy and the rest of the ladies was not going to be easy. First, we would let the ladies think that their prank had worked. Second, we would play a trick on the ladies by actually showing up at the therapist's office. But this time, we would be dressed in the same manner as the canines did when they had their therapy session and as an added bonus, each of the men would use an improvised script. That alone would send the therapist to seek help. I picked up the therapist's business card and said to the men *"Do you think that this woman is a real therapist?"* The men looked at the business card and agreed that the ladies must be using someone they hired to play the part. There are not too many therapists that have their photos on their business card that portray them as a blond goddess. I looked at the men and said *"Come on guys. Therapists don't look that good."* In addition, once we acted out the prank, Marty would go home and tell his wife of the dreadful evening he had and place the blame on me for the pranks. As a tribute for our well thought-out plan, we would have a group photo taken and send it to the local news office with the caption reading *"Group Spoils Potential Prank."*

Harry looked at me and said *"Okay. Let's get to work."* After the men wrote their scripts for the therapist session, I told Marty to take off his shirt. He looked at me and said *"Hey pal, I am not that kind of guy."* Even Rick had to add his version of a jovial statement when he said *"I might be one who likes strip-o-grams but not this kind."* Not to be outdone by my comrades, I smiled at the gang and said *"Don't worry. Marty can't carry a tune."* Marty hesitantly placed his shirt on the chair. I instructed my pal to stand back as I placed the hour glass on the table in front of the shirt and flipped the timer. Within moments, a fiery red blast hit its intended target. I then placed the shirt in another chair for the dye to set in. Just as I was about to get another shirt for Marty, the door-bell rang. Adam arrived in the nick of time. Beth had hired him to judge the men's contest. When he saw that Marty had his shirt off, he jokingly said to the gang *"If I thought I was going to judge a strip-tease show, I would have brought another bottle of Scotch."* I quickly explained to our dear friend the prank his beloved daughter-in-law had intended for the men.

When Adam placed that beautiful bottle of Scotch on the table, we all knew it was going to be a very long and enjoyable evening. Rick once again rubbed his hands in excitement as he reached for the bottle. Adam said to Rick *"You haven't won it yet."* and placed the bottle in a secure box. Instead, he placed a recording device on the table as it was going to be proof for the ladies that the contest actually took place. It was as if a dream came true. We used the recording device to our advantage and staged a series of pranks so that the ladies will think their plan worked. To start the show, Marty began reading the first story. On cue, Marty playfully shouted out *"Oh no, I can't believe the hour glass exploded. I have red dye all over me."* To continue with the prank, we sent Harry Sr. into the bathroom after we installed the clacker device. Once again and on cue, Harry Sr. lifted the toilet seat. Everyone heard a loud scream coming from the bathroom. It was followed by Harry Sr.'s voice yelling *"Who did this? It scared the crap out of me."* As soon as the rest of the men finished with their scripts, Adam shut off the recording device. I said to the men *"That should hold the ladies for a while."*

Meanwhile, back at the ladies headquarters, or Cindy's house, the ladies were enjoying their evening. Beth and Brenda arrived in time for another round of margaritas. Brenda told Cindy *"The package has been delivered."* as if she was reading a script from a movie. The ladies of course gave her and Beth high-fives as they spent the rest of the evening planning the event at the therapist office.

For the men, well, at least we thought that our plan would work, as long as Marty's acting abilities held up when he went home. After we went over the final script, Marty made the comment *"We will show the ladies who is boss."* Adam at this point could only shrug his shoulders and said to Marty *"I do hope you know a good divorce lawyer."* Of course Adam was paid handsomely for his efforts that night in exchange for the tape. It was all up to Marty.

Cindy was sitting in the living room reading a book when Marty arrived home. She sent the ladies home early so that she would be the first to hear about the men's poker night and their night of disaster. Marty walked in the front door determined to play his part. He saw that his wife was still up and said *"Hi honey. How was your night?"* Before

Cindy could respond, Marty removed his jacket exposing the popular stain we placed on his shirt. Pretending to be shocked, Cindy shouted *"Oh no. What happened dear?"* Marty sat across from his wife and told her of the dreadful evening he had with the men and the pranks that I played on him. He even said *"I can't believe the Author did this to me. My best friend."* Marty also added how I had played a prank on Harry Sr. and how the clacker device scared him so much that Harry Sr. lost his appetite. Cindy was doing her best to refrain from laughing out loud and telling her husband of her plan to get even with the men. Marty continued with his acting role and told Cindy *"I can't wait until the morning. We will get even with the Author if it's the last thing we do."*

In playing the supportive wife like she always does, Cindy placed her arm around her husband and emphatically told him that he would feel better after a hot shower. As he was heading up the stairs, Cindy commented *"Maybe you should get another best friend."* Angrily, Marty shouted down to his wife and said *"Oh no, that would be too good for him. I have other plans for that prankster."* Cindy immediately grabbed her cell-phone and contacted Brenda. She told her partner in crime that the plan was working. She even called Harriett to confirm Marty's story as well as Eve. Eve told Cindy that the Author scared her husband so much that he wanted to go on a diet. That comment alone made Eve mad as she further told Cindy that she wanted her man back, disgusting as he was. Cindy then called Beth to make sure the second part of their plan was in place. Beth told the leader that the therapist was on board with the plan and would deliver the tape to her on Sunday. Between the tape Adam possessed and the tape of the therapy session, Beth and Brenda would surely have one great story for the next book, at the expense of the men.

Marty woke up the next morning in a cheerful mood. When he joined his wife for their morning coffee together, Cindy was a little surprised that her husband was in a cheerful mood after the disastrous evening he had. She said *"How can you be in a cheerful mood after last night?"* Marty poured himself a cup of coffee, gave his wife a refill and said *"Time to get even, not mad."* He then told his beloved queen that he was going to meet the guys at the coffee shop and plan a revenge prank. One prank, according to Marty, that would be listed as the prank of a lifetime. He even told Cindy *"By the time we get done with the Author, he will be looking for a sense of humor in another country."* Yep, I will say this. Marty certainly knows how to act. He took one final sip of his coffee and kissed his wife on the cheek. As he left the house, Marty told Cindy that he had an errand to run after the meeting at the coffee shop. Out of sight from Cindy, Marty sent me a text message that read *"On my way. The goose is in the oven."*

The rest of the men were seated at the round table when Marty arrived at my house. We were going over the scripts and the outfits that we were going to wear. I once again pulled out book three and told the gang the outfits that were worn by the pet characters. Rick was the first to ask *"Who is going to be whom?"* Before I could brief the

men on their pet character roles, the door-bell rang. Ralph
arrived in time to give us much needed information about
the therapist and the layout of her office. I had told the
men that I sent Ralph on a scouting mission that morning.
Ralph placed the photos on the table and handed me the
bag of clothes to be worn by the men. He said to me *"I hope
you know what you are doing."* As Ralph was leaving the
room, he turned to Marty and said *"By the way, in case you
don't make it, can I have your baseball card collection?"*

Now it was time to answer Rick's question on who
was going to be whom. I grabbed a pair of over-sized
sunglasses, a polo shirt, neon-green pants and flip-flops
and handed them to Harry. Smiling, I told Harry that he
was going to portray his former pet Mr. High Pockets.
In addition to the garments, I gave Harry that trusted
flame-thrower with instructions to shoot water only. For
Marty, I gave him an outfit that made him look like a
gunslinger. He would portray himself as an outlaw,
dressed in black and packing those ever-so-popular six
shooters. His instructions were to shoot strawberry jam
only. I then looked at Harry Sr. and handed him a bib.
He looked at me and said *"Is this the only thing you want
me to wear?"* I am sure that if the men allowed Harry Sr.
to walk into a therapist's office wearing nothing but a
bib, the ladies would have our heads on a silver platter.
Finally, I handed Rick his costume. With the instructions
that he would act out a series of pranks, Rick would be
wearing shorts, sandals and a blond wig. The wig of course
was representative of his old pet Lulu. Now that the men

had their outfits, we proceeded to the therapist's office. According to Marty, this was one day that the therapist wished she would have called in sick.

Miss Wagner was the therapist that, according to Beth, would be the only therapist that could conduct a counseling session on such short notice. When we arrived at the office building, Rick went to the listing on the wall to see what floor our therapist's office was on. At first Rick was confused because he noticed that there were two Miss Wagner's listed on the same floor. He said to himself *"Guess it doesn't matter which one we see."* Rick then told us the office number as we huddled in the elevator thinking of our poor therapist. Marty once again said *"She won't know what hit her."* It was the first office located across from the elevator. We walked in to the office as if we had a scheduled appointment and a much needed one at that. When I told the young receptionist my name and the appointment time, she looked concerned as she said *"Are you sure? Miss Wagner has no appointment scheduled."* I handed her the therapist's business card with the appointment time. The receptionist confirmed that it was Miss Wagner so she called the therapist to see if she was willing to hold a counseling session since her next appointment was not for another 2 hours. When the receptionist got off the phone, she told us that Miss Wagner would see us in a moment and for us to make ourselves comfortable.

I will hand it to Ralph. The layout of the office was exactly as he had portrayed it to be. I was a little concerned as to why our appointment was not listed in Miss Wagner's appointment book. To the men, it did not matter. It did not take long for the therapist to emerge from her office. I could see that the men were excited as their glares told me that the therapist was a knock out. At first glance, I noticed she wore a stunning business outfit that captured every essence of her body. Except for the change in her hair color and the lack of glasses, she did look similar to the photo on her business card. I told the therapist that I was there for the appointment and that the rest of the men were there for support. As I followed the stunning therapist to her office, I looked back at Harry Sr. and said *"Stop drooling and use your bib."* Rick was heard saying *"Why does he get to go first?"*

Miss Wagner had me sit in a chair across from hers. She provocatively sat down and after crossing her legs, the young therapist asked me how she could help with my problem. First, I told the therapist that I was needing guidance because of recurring dreams I was having. I then said *"On top of that, my friends think that I am going crazy and need help."* Miss Wagner jotted down a few notes and as any therapist would do, she asked questions that pertained to one's childhood. Since I was living up to my part as being the crazy one, I told the therapist that the session was supposed to be a group session. Miss Wagner's eyes widened when she heard my comment and then asked me *"So you say that you think the adult characters are crazy and not you?"* I nodded my head in agreement and told the therapist that I can prove to her that the adult characters needed help and not me. As I opened the door to motion the men to join the session, I told the therapist *"Wait until you analyze these clowns. You will see."*

All the men sat directly across from the therapist except Harry Sr. He placed a small chair in the center of the room and then as on cue, began the task of setting the stage for the first of what was to come. Harry Sr. then reached into his bag and placed a small plate of Eve's lasagna on a small nightstand in front of him. Next, he gently placed dinner settings on the table and donned the bib. By now, all eyes were on Harry Sr. When he noticed the quietness of the office, he looked up and saw everyone staring at him, including the therapist. He said *"Hey, don't look at me. I just drove these nut jobs here."* This scene was undoubtedly a first for the young therapist. She placed her hand over her eyes not believing what was taking place in her office. It took a moment for her to regain her composure. When she cleared her throat, the therapist said to me *"I can see your point."* Rick noticed that the therapist had shaken her head in disbelief. I nodded to Rick to start the next phase of our prank.

As soon as he rose from his seat, Rick adjusted his shorts and looked around the room. He saw a large plant standing in the corner of the room. Just like his old pet Lulu, Rick smiled and made a bee-line for the plant. Without hesitation, Rick dropped his shorts and marked his territory. When he finished, Rick sat down and said *"Oh what a relief that was."* Seeing that the therapist's mouth was wide open, Rick acted out the second part of his role. He jumped from his seat and sat on the therapist's desk, crossed his legs and caressed the wig that made him look ten years younger. Rick grabbed the small jar of jelly beans that was centered on the therapist's desk, leaned toward Miss Wagner and said *"These are good. Let me know if you want the good stuff. I can hook you up."* Once again the young therapist could not believe what was happening. By now, she must have been thinking that her therapy session had turned into a circus act. She blurted out *"What next? Bobbing for apples."*

Harry and Marty looked at each other trying to decide who was going to be the next actor to mesmerize our young therapist. Harry took it upon himself to act out the prank. He stood in front of the therapist, reached behind him and displayed Mr. High Pocket's flame-thrower. Suddenly Harry shouted *"Flame on."* and sent a large stream of water in the direction of Miss Wagner. As soon as the effect of the water blast left its mark, Miss Wagner stood and screamed as if she was shot. I looked at Harry and said sarcastically *"Harry how could you? You should be ashamed of yourself."* Seeing that the therapist needed comforting as well as a dry towel, I saw to it that Miss Wagner had ample time to dry off so that we could continue with our session. After I apologized to the therapist for Harry's behavior, I grabbed another towel from my bag. This time, it was my popular roll of the "Glow in the Dark" paper towels. Without hesitation, the therapist grabbed the towels and wiped off her face and neck. Clearing her throat, Miss Wagner said *"Let's continue with the session, shall we?"*

Marty stood up and faced the therapist. With a southern accent, he began a unique dialogue that certainly came from an old western movie. First he said *"Us cowpokes have a saying in this here parts."* Miss Wagner was slightly amused at what Marty said as she asked him *"So, tell us what you cowpokes say."* Smiling, Marty placed both hands on his six-shooters and said *"Make my day."* He quickly drew the guns and fired two shots at the therapist, both hitting its mark. Miss Wagner's white blouse was covered in strawberry jam. Once he re-holstered his guns, Marty added *"Let that be a lesson to you. Never mess with a cowpoke."* For the second time the young therapist stood angry at what the men did to her. Before she could orally display her disgust, the men took it upon themselves to act out their own roles at the same time. It was what they proverbially called the straw that broke the camel's back. At the top of her lungs, Miss Wagner shouted *"Get out of my office. All of you."* while pointing to the door. Since I was the last one to leave the office, I asked the therapist if we were going to be charged full price for the session. When I saw that the therapist grabbed the empty glass container that once held her jelly beans, I knew I better leave before that glass container found its mark.

We left the building with our health intact. A job well done for a group of men who each proclaim to have a sense of humor. Marty still had one small role to play when he arrived home. He had to convince Cindy that he and the rest of the men were satisfied in performing a future revenge prank. Cindy did find it strange that her husband's attitude was slightly different than what it was when he first left the house that morning. As soon as Marty went upstairs to take his mid-afternoon nap, Cindy called Brenda and asked her if she had heard from the therapist. She told the queen that there was no word from the therapist. This was good news for the men, or at least in their eyes no news is good news. Now that both events were complete, I sent a text message to Beth to let her know that we could meet at the coffee shop Monday morning to exchange envelopes and reveal the winners of the contest.

The Showdown

Patiently waiting for the ladies to arrive, Marty and I went over the final script. This was definitely one time the men had the upper hand on the ladies. It was great knowing that Cindy could be beaten at her own game. I looked at Marty and said *"Are you sure you are up to this?"* A grin from Marty told me he was indeed ready. Ready to drop the hammer on the ladies and their so-called prank. Marty placed his cell-phone on the table so that he could capture the moment when the ladies heard that their plot had been foiled. According to him, it would be a Kodak moment. Yep, Marty was certainly ready.

As soon as I saw the ladies enter the coffee shop, I nudged Marty and said *"Okay pal, we're on."* We rose from our seats to greet the ladies in a gentlemanly fashion that men are most famous for. There we stood, side by side, waiting for the ladies to approach the table. Another classic scene from a western movie. When Beth and Cindy saw us standing in front of the table, they hesitated as the ladies did not expect us to appear in such a forgiving mood. After all, to them, they thought they had the upper hand and had performed such a prank that would go down in history as the prank that taught the men a final lesson. If I was a betting man, I would say that Cindy probably had a dream on how she would write her own book on how to save other women from pranks conducted by their husbands. When the ladies finally approached the table, Marty whispered to me *"Look at them. They think they won."* Once the pleasantries were exchanged, I asked Beth *"Do you have the package?"* With her flirtatious smile, she placed a sealed envelope on the table. I placed the sealed envelope from Adam on the table as well. All four of us stared at the envelopes wondering who was going to be the first to break down and discuss the events of the contest.

I pushed Adam's envelope in Beth's direction and said *"Ladies' first."* Beth opened the envelope and showed the results to Cindy. She blurted out *"I should have known."* as the winner of the men's contest was Marty. Marty said to the ladies *"That's right. Back on the throne again. I expect the trophy to be delivered to my house today."* Beth smiled and told Marty that the contest was conditional in that we needed proof that the men saw the therapist. Grinning as always and still in control of the situation, Marty told the ladies that we had proof. He looked at me and said *"Go ahead and give them the tape.*" I placed the tape on the table. Before the ladies conceded to the fact that the men won their bet, Marty said *"You have all the proof you need on that tape and then some."* As the ladies gave each other a puzzled look, Marty took it upon himself to reveal Cindy's plot. He said to his wife *"The jig is up honey. We knew what you ladies were planning all along."* It was at this point I should have expressed my concerns to Marty and tell him to stop talking. Instead, I allowed Marty to ramble on and tell the ladies of the pranks we pulled on the therapist that the ladies had hired. Finally, Marty crossed his arms, leaned back in his chair and said *"So you see, we are still Kings of our castles."*

Beth could only smile at Marty as she felt that the smirk he was portraying on his face needed to be changed and changed in a hurry. She gave Marty an evil glare and said *"Really."* Beth then reached into her bag and placed a newspaper on the table. Her eyes widened with anticipation when she asked us *"Is this the therapist you went to see?"* and pointed to a photo on the front page of the newspaper. Marty quickly responded *"Yep. One in the same."* Our smiles soon turned to horror as Marty and I read the front-page story. It depicted a therapist that went on a rampage in a building and eventually got arrested for destroying her office. There was one photo of the therapist being hauled away in handcuffs with her saying *"They made me do it."* After a brief description of the events was a photo of the men. It was the photo I sent in to the newspaper of the men clad in our outfits that was taken outside her office.

To take the heat off Marty, I reminded Beth that Miss Wagner was the therapist she sent us to and placed her business card on the table. Still smiling, she said *"By the way, where was her office located?"* When I told Beth that the therapist office was located across from the elevator, she once again smiled and said *"You guys went to the wrong therapist. Our Miss Wagner has her office down the hall."* Befuddled and bewildered was not a true emotion Marty and I were feeling when the proverbial hammer was dropped on our toes. The ladies rose from their seat thanking us for a fine story. Beth said *"By the way, since you went to the wrong therapist, the men's contest is null and void."* Cindy then tore up the envelope with her husband's name on it, placed the pieces in his shirt pocket and said *"Better luck next time."* Beth then grabbed the sealed envelope which contained the results of the ladies contest and said *"I better hold on to this. After all, I would not want anything to happen to the ladies' night of glory."*

When the ladies left the coffee shop, I called the rest of the gang to break the bad news. Harry, Rick and Harry Sr. arrived at the shop just as disgusted as Marty and I were. When Rick asked me what happened, I replied *"You did."* and showed him the front-page story of our beloved therapist. Marty then said to him *"Next time wear your glasses."* Before we could figure out our next move, Sophie walked into the coffee shop. Grinning, she said *"Yep, just as I thought. Five morons for the price of one."* She took out her camera and snapped several photos. Harry asked her why she was taking photos of the men. Sophie told us that

Cindy called her and wanted the photos. Marty asked Sophie *"Why? So she can rub it in our faces later on."* Sophie said no and that Cindy wanted the photos for a book that she was writing. I said *"Really! What's the name of the book?"* Without looking up, Sophie replied *"The Book of Morons."*

SOPHIE WINS THE LOTTERY: FINALLY

Hooray, Sophie finally won the Lottery. Yeah, right. Like that's ever going to happen. A canine winning the Lottery. Not in the real world. Now let's imagine this for a moment. A man walks into a local convenient store with his pet. He walks up to the counter and tells the clerk that he wants to buy a Lottery ticket for his dog. At first glance, the clerk thinks that the man is either off his rocker or had been drinking. Regardless, a sale is a sale so the clerk accepts the money and prints out a ticket. After he hands the man his Lottery ticket, the man places the ticket in a pouch that is attached to his dog's collar and says *"There you go pal."* If the man did win the Lottery, he would of course be given money in the form of a check. That is after Uncle Sam takes their cut. In the realm of the "No Sense of Humor" series, the scenario would be slightly different.

Canines don't use paper money. If they did, most of them would use it to line Daisy Mae's bird cage or use it in a more popular fashion similar to what the adult characters would use when potty training their puppies. Some even read the fine print and enjoy making jokes with their fellow canines about the photos. To the canines, paper money was useless. In their minds, winning the Lottery meant winning a vast amount of dog biscuits. After all, dog biscuits are the only items canines can use. They use it buy novelties, entice other canines to pull pranks as well as host parties. At least that's what the canines used in the beginning. Now that the series has evolved and the canines have adapted their own unique lifestyle, the canines decided to improve their way of life.

I decided to stop at Ralph's store the morning after the ladies title-quest was finished to find out from Beth when we were going to announce the winner. She was busy at her desk working on a new story-line when I said *"So Beth, when are we going to have the ceremony?"* Beth replied *"Soon, I hope. I am waiting for the ladies to tell me when they can all be together."* She then told me that she was glad that I was at the store. Beth mentioned that when she was reviewing the story-line that there was plenty of free space that needed to be filled up before the book went to print. She said *"Remember the story you wrote on Banking with Canines."* I told Beth I remembered the story quite well. My writing assistant wrote two words on a piece of paper and handed it to me. I asked Beth what it was and she replied *"An idea for a new story."* The words printed on the paper said *"Canine Money"*. After I told Beth that she had a great idea, she responded *"Good. Now get to work and leave me alone. I have work to do myself."* When I got home, I set up my lap-top and poured myself a cup of coffee. Thinking of the story I was about to write made me hungry. I noticed that Sophie was in the kitchen making her usual bacon and eggs and asked her if she could make me a sandwich. Sophie growled at me but went to work on my sandwich. I could tell that she was still not happy so I said to her *"Sophie, this is your lucky day."* and then added *"You might win the Lottery."* Sophie jumped for joy and said to me *"It's about time you came to your senses."* While Sophie was busy making her list of what items she wanted to buy, I went to work on my lap-top to write the story. I didn't have the heart to tell her that first she needed to buy a ticket and that the odds of actually winning the Lottery was the same as if Ralph became a history professor.

Mr. High Pocket's job as the Mayor of Dogville certainly has earned him a lot of praise and respect. He spends his days working on problems presented to him by the canine community. The "Yapper" formed a canine council to help him with the needs of the community. This council met in his office every Monday morning. Leaders from various organizations as well as Ralph and Tom were part of this council. On one particular Monday, Mr. High Pockets wanted to present to the council a plan he created that would fix a problem that endangered the growth of the canine community; shortage of dog biscuits. Ralph and Tom always arrived early to give Mr. High Pockets their canine version of opinions before the other leaders arrived. While they were enjoying their friendly bantering, Mr. High Pockets received a gift from an anonymous person.

It was a very large array of flowers expertly displayed in a colorful vase. The card that was attached to the gift read *"Keep up the good work. We love what you are doing for us. Signed, Anonymous."*

Tom jokingly whispered to Ralph *"I wonder if he has a girlfriend. Must be that cutie that works in accounting."* Before Ralph and Tom could muster a few jokes about the "Yapper's" gift, the Mayor's secretary announced that the remaining members of the council would be late because they were stuck in traffic. So, Mr. High Pocket's decided to start the meeting without them. He called the meeting to order and announced the first business at hand. After informing Ralph and Tom of the latest problem, Mr. High Pocket's asked Ralph if he was having any kind of problem at his store. Ralph told the Mayor that business was slow and that many of his long-time canine customers could not afford the novelties because of the shortage of dog biscuits. Tom jokingly blurted out *"Yeah, too bad we can't use human money. At least the canines would get a big laugh."* Suddenly that old proverbial light-bulb flashed above Ralph's head. He turned to Tom and said *"Tom, that's it. You are a genius."*

Looking at Ralph as if he was on the Author's Prozac, Mr. High Pocket's said *"Been hitting the Prozac again?"* Ralph ignored the comment and then told the council his idea. He said that they could create canine money to replace the dog biscuits. Ralph also added that the city could host the first-ever canine Lottery where one dog biscuit would buy two canine Lottery tickets. Mr. High

Pocket's liked the idea but told Ralph that it would cost the city too much money to start such an operation. He told the council that there was not enough money in the budget to buy a new printing press let alone rent out a facility. Once again Ralph came up with another idea. He said *"We can do it at my house. I have a printing press, remember?"* Once the canines worked out the details of their new project, Mr. high Pocket's began working on the press release.

Ralph and Tom worked out the details for the printing of the canine money on the ride home. First, they would move the printing press into the same room where Ralph has his hot-tub. Then, since he was also a cartoonist, Ralph would draw a design of the various pet characters in the books and use their photos on the canine money. The more popular the canine, the more valuable the currency. I guess you can add cartoonist to Ralph's already impressive resume. Pixy and Dixy would help at the house when they were not guarding Daisy Mae. The duo would also print up the fliers to advertise the canine lottery. Canines throughout the community would be able to use their current dog biscuits to purchase the lottery tickets or us the new canine currency once their biscuits were exchanged. After informing their spouses of their brilliant plan to save the community, Ralph and Tom went to work and set up their improved printing press.

The next morning I received a call from Ralph. He informed me that he had started a new project and wanted to share it with me. I arrived at Ralph's house thinking to myself *"What in the world has Ralph gotten himself into now."* Ralph greeted me at the door and escorted me to the printing press. He said *"See, we are making money."* I looked at Ralph and said *"Do you know what we humans call it?"* Before Ralph could answer I added *"It's called counterfeiting."* and quickly told my publisher that it normally carries a very long prison sentence. Ralph told me not to worry and that they were not making human money. He handed me a printing plate and then told me of the plan the council came up with to save the community. When I saw the photos of the pet characters he planned on printing on the canine currency, I jokingly said to Ralph *"At least you are not making No Sense of Humor money."* Ralph placed his paw on my shoulder and said with a grin *"We don't have time. Besides, I am saving that for the next book."* Still not sure that my trusted canine knew what he was getting into, I reached into his closet, grabbed his old bus-boy uniform and headed out the door. Ralph shouted *"Hey boss. Where are you going with my uniform?"* I shouted back *"To have it changed into pin-stripes, just in case."*

I left Ralph's house still shaking my head and thought about the comment Ralph made about the "No Sense of Humor" money. If Ralph was serious, I could only imagine what would take place at the canine's next poker night if Ralph printed the money that would have the faces of all of the adult male characters. Soon, the scenario whisked through my mind. I imagined Ralph and Tom sitting at their round table, each holding cards in their paws ready to place their bets. Ralph would say *"Tom, I bet you four*

Marty's, two Rick's and a Harry." Tom of course would reply
"I will see your bet and raise you four Harry's and four Zeke's."
I shook my head to erase that thought from my mind and
headed home to tell Sophie of the news. Sophie was so
elated about the news that she brought out her canine
bank and counted all of the dog biscuits she had saved.
She wanted to exchange the biscuits right away but I told
my beloved pet that Ralph needed time to print the canine
money. She asked me about the lottery and when she was
going to win. I told her that the fliers will be up this week
announcing where canines can go to buy their tickets.

Meanwhile, Annie was sitting at her desk at the Cat
Mafia headquarters discussing her latest endeavors with
Amy on the phone. Amy was not pleased with what had
recently taken place and begged Annie to try to find a
way to get rid of the canines. As soon as Annie was off
the phone with Amy, one of her henchmen walked into
her office and told her that he delivered the package as
ordered. Annie had sent her henchmen to deliver the
flower arrangement that now proudly sits on Mr. High
Pockets' desk but with a listening device attached under
the vase. She said to her henchmen *"Let's see what those
flea-bitten brats have been up too."* Annie plugged in the
receiver portion to her lap-top and intently listed to the
conversations that took place during Mr. High Pocket's
council meeting. When she found out about the plan to
print canine money, Annie immediately called Amy with
the good news. Together, they discussed a plan to once
again foil the attempts by the canines. This time, the Cat

Mafia would print money of their own and use it to replace the lottery money. Once the winner would be announced, Annie would hold a press conference about the corrupt nature of the lottery and place the blame on Mr. High Pocket's, therefore ending his career as Mayor.

Not only would Annie's plan end Mr. High Pocket's career, but it would also endanger the lives and careers of any canines that were associated with the lottery plan, mainly Ralph and Tom. First, Annie needed to obtain the printing plates from Ralph's house. Once she had the plates then Annie would have her henchmen print the phony money. To her, it was feline currency since the canine photos would be replaced by members of her organization. Then she would convert one of her warehouses into a lottery center ran by the Cat Mafia. After the lottery, Annie would then hold her own press conference and expose the corruption of the phony money used by the canines. All Annie would have to do once the entire plan was executed was watch the local news to enjoy seeing the canines being taken to prison.

After surveying Ralph's house, the Cat Mafia henchmen picked a day where they could steal the printing plates from the canines. It was on a Monday and since it was the first day of the work-week, the henchmen knew that Ralph and Tom would be at the store. Penny always left for work early on Monday's to conduct inventories before opening the store. Mary Ann did her shopping once the children were in school. This left two canines to guard the house; Pixy and Dixy. Once the henchmen saw that everyone had left the house, one waited in the van across the street while the other delivered a package. The henchmen hoped that Pixy or Dixy would answer the door. He was in luck. Pixy opened the door and asked the disguised delivery canine what he wanted. The henchmen said *"I have a delivery for Pixy and Dixy from a Ralph M. Esquire."* Pixy saw that the package contained donuts and called out to Dixy *"We got a package from Ralph."* Pixy signed for the package and as he was about to close the door, the delivery guy extended his hand as if he was expecting a tip. Dixy saw the gesture and said jokingly *"Oh, don't bet on Princess in the fourth. She just had a litter a few weeks ago."* The henchmen went back to the van and said to himself *"What a cheap Moron."*

Pixy and Dixy returned to the workshop determined to devour the donuts. Pixy said to his partner *"So, what do we do first? Eat or work?"* To Dixy, the answer was a no-brainer. Within minutes, the young Dobermans ate the entire box of donuts. It didn't take long for the canines to fall asleep. The henchmen that had delivered the package looked at his watch and said to his partner *"They should be asleep by now."* He had placed a large amount of sleeping pills inside the donuts. Both henchmen then went inside the house to execute what Annie called "Plan A". One of the henchmen replaced the canine printing plates with their own while the other kept a look-out in case one of the canines decided to come home early. After the henchmen had printed two bags of feline cash, they replaced the printing plates with the canine's plates and hid the feline plates under the press. One of the henchmen said to the other as they were leaving *"I don't understand why we can't beat these guys. They are so easy."*

Ralph and Tom went home that evening unaware of the events that had taken place earlier in the day. Pixy and Dixy were not about to thank Ralph for the donuts since they fell asleep on the job. It appeared to Ralph and Tom that there was enough money that had been printed to make the exchange at the Bank of Canines the following morning as well as ensure there were ample funds made available for the lottery. Tom took the remaining funds to the Lottery center. Mr. High Pocket's held his press conference in front of City Hall. Soon, canines throughout the community went to various convenient stores to purchase lottery tickets. When I told Sophie that she needed to buy her Lottery tickets, she re-counted her dog biscuits and headed straight to the nearest convenient store. In passing she said *"Thanks boss for letting me win the Lottery."* I told my beloved pet that she hadn't won yet as it was just a game of chance.

The Lottery for canines was just a game of chance. Canines viewed this as a way of escaping their financial problems. Others perceived it as a chance to get rich. Sophie hoped to win the Lottery so that she could pay off the debts she created from her shopping spree. On the day of the drawing, Sophie invited Ralph and Tom to the house to witness her winning the Lottery. Or, brag about how rich she was going to be. I told Sophie *"Don't count your chickens until they hatch."* Tom, once again not

understanding certain proverbial phrases said to Sophie
"*Chickens. I didn't know you had chickens. Is that why you
make a lot of bacon and eggs?*" I shook my head and watched
as the canines turned on the TV to view the winning
numbers. When the winning numbers were displayed, as
luck would have it, Sophie had the winning ticket. She
jumped for joy and danced around the room yelling "*I am
rich. I am rich.*" After she bragged about how she was going
to spend her newfound wealth, Sophie treated the canines
to lunch.

After lunch, Sophie went to the Lottery center to claim
her prize. When the henchman saw Sophie walk into
the center, he knew she was the so-called winner of the
Lottery. He said to himself "*Yep, there is a sucker born every
minute.* Sophie handed the clerk her ticket and told him
that she was the winner. He scanned the ticket through
the computer and when the numbers matched, he said
to Sophie "*Congratulations. You are the jackpot winner.*"
He handed Sophie two large bags of cash and asked the
Lottery winner if she would mind posing for a photo. Of
course Sophie would never turn down an opportunity
to be the center of attention. She said to herself "*This
will look great on my Facebook page.*" Once her so-called
photo session was done, Sophie went to the department
store to pay off her debt. She took a wad of the Lottery
cash from the bag and handed it to the clerk. At first, the
clerk was surprised to see Sophie since my beloved canine
had another two weeks before her first payment was due.
Considering the value of the money Sophie gave the clerk,

the clerk told Sophie that she had to go to the back room to check out the currency and then print out a receipt. The clerk placed the money under a fluorescent light and said to herself *"Oh my. This is not good."* and immediately called the fraud hotline.

When the clerk returned to give Sophie her receipt, she told my beloved canine that there was a problem printing out her receipt and that the problem should be fixed within a few minutes. Suddenly, two federal agents walked in the door. The lead agent said to Sophie *"Are you Sophie Marie Morgan."* as he displayed his badge. When Sophie said yes, the agent told her that she needed to go with them and placed her in handcuffs. Sophie shouted *"What is going on here?"* The lead agent escorted Sophie to an awaiting van and said to her *"You are under arrest. For possession of counterfeit money."* This was one time my beloved canine was speechless. During the booking process, the agents told Sophie that she was allowed to make a phone call. Sophie wasn't about to call me considering she probably thought that it was my fault that she was arrested. Instead she called Samantha. Sophie knew that Samantha would be the only pet character that could save her.

Samantha didn't waste any time in answering Sophie's call. When she arrived at the jail-house, Sophie pleaded with Samantha to investigate what happened. She told the FBI agent that she didn't do it and that she was framed. Samantha asked Sophie *"Where did you get the money?"* Sophie told Samantha that she picked up the cash at the Lottery Center when she won the Lottery. Even though Samantha felt that Sophie was telling the truth, Samantha told Sophie that her story needed to be checked out considering the amount of evidence that was against her. Sophie replied *"Wait until we get there. You will see."* Samantha placed Sophie into her custody and with two other agents, drove Sophie to the Lottery Center. When they arrived, Samantha noticed that there was no sign that the building had been used as a Lottery Center. Sophie said *"I don't know either but the clerk inside will remember me. I had my photo taken there too."* Sophie's jaw dropped to the floor when she and the agents walked in the door. Instead of a busy Lottery Center, they saw an old chair, an empty card-board box and an old phone lying on the floor. Since Sophie's story did not check out, Samantha was forced to return Sophie to jail.

On the way back to jail, the Director of the FBI called Samantha. He wanted her to return to the headquarters as there was a development in the case that needed her attention. As soon as Samantha walked in the Director's office, he said *"Take a look at this."* and turned on the TV to watch a special news bulletin. Shocked beyond belief, the agents saw Annie standing at the foot-steps to City Hall talking to news reporters. She was heard telling the press about the attempted cover-up by city officials regarding the Lottery. Annie showed several photos to the press, one of which was of Sophie Smiling while holding two bags of cash. Annie then said to a reporter. *"See, it pays to have friends in high places."* referring to Sophie's relationship with Mr. High Pockets. The Director gave Samantha a disgusted look and told her to start a complete investigation because for him it was turning into a political nightmare. After she left the Director's office, Samantha returned to the scene of the crime, mainly the old Lottery Center. She looked around for clues hoping to find something that would clear Sophie's name. Samantha found a photo lying on the floor and said to herself "*I hope this helps.*" Instead, she found a photo of Ralph and Tom shaking hands in front of their printing press, with Mr. High Pocket's holding a pair of printing plates. She said to herself "*This does not look good. What has Ralph gotten himself into this time?*"

Meanwhile, Ralph and Tom returned home to enjoy dinner with their families. They were happy that Sophie had won the Lottery. Neither one had heard the news about the potential Lottery scam. Ralph's TV was broken and the young pups were playing video games on Tom's TV. Half-way through dinner, Ralph heard a knock on the door. He was surprised to see that Samantha was at his house with two armed FBI agents. Startled by her presence, Ralph asked Samantha "*Hey Sam, what are you doing here?*" Samantha handed Ralph a search warrant and told him of the Lottery scam and of Sophie's arrest. She also told Ralph that even though she thinks that the Cat Mafia might be behind the scheme that her Director wanted her team to investigate the situation. Samantha then handed a copy of the photo that she had found at the crime scene and said "*It doesn't look good.*" While Ralph explained the Lottery plan to Samantha, the other agents feverishly searched Ralph's workshop. One of the agents approached Samantha and said *"I found these."* He handed the canine printing plates to the lead agent and Ralph said *"See, those are the ones we used."* The other agent called out to Samantha stating that he had found something under the printing press. When she went to see what the item was, the other agent handed a small bag to Samantha and said *"These were hidden under the press."* Samantha was shocked when she uncovered the phony plates.

Tom shouted *"Those aren't ours."* as he made his plea to the FBI agents that they did not know how the phony plates were in Ralph's house. The evidence was clear. Samantha had Sophie's photo, her bag of phony money, Ralph and Tom's photo along with the phony plates. She looked at Ralph and said *"Sorry pal, but I have no choice."* The agents placed handcuffs on Ralph and Tom and said *"You are both under arrest for counterfeiting."* Pixy and Dixy were also arrested as accomplices. Samantha then contacted two other agents to arrest Mr. High Pockets. Everyone in the room knew that Ralph and Tom were innocent but the evidence was certainly stacked against them. It appeared that this was one time that Ralph could not find a way out of trouble. Annie now had her much needed victory over the canines.

(To Be Continued).

UNANSWERED
QUESTIONS

For the men's next poker night, I decided to do something special for the men. It seemed that I picked a great time to give the men a much-deserved present. Earlier in the week, I had taken Ralph's suggestion and created a new novelty that would be used in the next book. The men felt that they were being neglected because of the ladies title-quest. In addition, since the ladies still could not make up their mind when they could be together to announce the winner of the title-quest, I told the men that I would be selecting the topic for our night of fun. I had sent an e-mail to each of the ladies in the form of a survey. The survey contained questions that were posed to them as if they were the ones creating the story-lines for the book. Not only did I want the ladies responses but I also wanted to hear the comments by the men once they read the survey, even though I don't have a sense of humor.

Despite the fact that the men were not involved in the ladies contest, they were still ready to banter and have fun.

Clad in their usual Friday-night outfits, the men arrived at my house ready to see what was in store for them. As usual, Marty prepared the drinks and Rick dealt the cards. Just as the last card was dealt, I announced to the gang that I had a present for them. I removed the poker chips from the table and placed a sealed box in the center. Smiling, I instructed Marty to open the box. At first he was hesitant afraid that I was about to pull a prank. I told my dear friend that pranks were not scheduled for our night of fun. Marty was still hesitant so I decided to open the box. I then neatly stacked the gifts in front of the men. They smiled when they saw that their poker chips had been replaced with "No Sense of Humor" money.

As each of my comrades rifled through their stack, I told the men to pay close attention to the photos on the bills. For Marty, I chose a photo from one of Cindy's stories. His bill showed Marty dressed in a pink apron while wearing Cindy's mittens. Rick shook his head when he saw his photo. I had his photo specially made. Included in his photo was a heart setting that contained Mindy's photo. Harry Sr. liked his photo. It was one of the original photos used to describe his character in the last book. The photo showed Harry Sr. holding up his stretchy pants. Little did Harry Sr. know that those very same pants ended up as a donation to a local charity, courtesy of Eve. Harry also liked his photo. His character was displayed without a smile while wearing a sweatshirt made by Harriett with a photo of Daisy Mae on the front. For myself, I went with a more professional look, the Author's photo.

After the normal bantering and comments of the photos were exchanged, the men gave me a look as if they were willing to accept a new tradition. Marty then asked me *"So, what is the value of each bill?"* I told Marty that each bill had the same value; none. Everyone but myself agreed that the bills should have some sort of value. As the discussion continued about what bills should have the greatest value, I told the men that they had plenty of time to discuss it at our next poker night. I then placed a copy of the results of the ladies' survey in front of the men and said *"This is our topic for tonight."* When Marty read the survey, he said *"I rather play with the money."* Rick then asked me why I had the ladies fill out the survey instead of the men. I told Rick that the story-line still evolved around the ladies. In keeping with tradition, I told the men *"Maybe I will give you guy's one in the next book provided you have a sense of humor."* So, according to my survey, this is the ladies version of "Unanswered Questions".

What one story would you pick to revise and why?

From what you have already learned about the series, I have written several revision stories. Most were kept the same but a few contained an added twist. The ladies chose stories that they knew could be re-written for their benefit. Or as Brenda and Bertha stated, put the shoe on the other foot. In the original "Psycho Kitties" story, Harriett would have had Harry kidnapped by the Cat Mafia instead of her. She also would have used a mechanical bird to replace Daisy Mae first rather than after the fact. After Beth and Brenda read the revised story on the novelties, they came up with the idea to revise part of the story that involved the use of Cindy's bra. If Cindy would have known that her husband was going to use her bra as beer coolers, she would have attached the clacker device to her bra. It may not have prevented Marty from ultimately using the bra, but it certainly would scare the daylights out of him. Cindy would have loved the chance to revise the story in which the ladies ended up soaking wet thanks to the mechanical water slide. Instead of Marty taking the ladies on a tour, she would be the one conducting the tour. Cindy claimed that the photos alone would be of great value to everyone's Facebook page.

One story that Bertha wanted to see revised was the one in which Cindy and Susan gave birth to twins. Even though Cindy foiled Jack's attempted prank, Bertha wanted to add her version of pranks on Jack and then again on Marty when he arrived home. The men felt the same way when it came down to the pranks that had been played on them. When Beth was first introduced as the writing assistant, Marty and Harry would have preferred to have the prank pulled on any of the ladies, as long as it was not them. Rest assure the men are now dreading their prankster days now that the ladies have had their way with them in this book.

Should the men be allowed to
judge another beauty contest?

If it was left up to me, I would let the men have another crack at judging a beauty contest. However, the ladies felt quite differently. The majority of the responses from the ladies were simply stated in two words, *"Heck No."* Included in Cindy's response was a request for the ladies to judge a beauty contest of their own. Her version would consist of five men that would parade in front of the ladies wearing nothing but tight shorts. To her and the rest of the ladies, they could care less if the men had brains, as long as each of the contestants was built like Adonis. Beth was asked by Cindy to create a story for her so that she can add it to her list for the next book. I am sure Bertha would enjoy the opportunity to use her latex gloves in that story. Of course the men would object to the women's night of pleasure. Comments that I heard from the men were *"Not in this lifetime.", "No way Jose."* and *"What do they need those hunks for? They have us."*

What should be written to
show Amy's whereabouts?

According to Cindy's e-mail, Amy was in a place where she belonged; out of sight and out of mind. The rest of the ladies wanted me to bring her back in the next book so that they could teach her a valuable lesson. They must have forgotten that Amy used to run her own novelty business and has read all of the books. Beth thought that if I brought back Amy that too many stories would be written to show how easily the men could be intimidated by her good looks. If this question would have been asked in the previous book, the answer would be obvious. Keep Amy in another country and allow the pet characters to gain prominence over the Cat Mafia by defeating Amy's twin-sister Annie. This statement certainly came true in the ladies recent title-quest. If it were up to the men, they would have me bring back Amy as well as Tonya and Sonya. Sarcastically I told the men *"Sure, let's put them in a beauty contest for the men and host the contest at Marty's house."*

Will the Author ever develop a sense of humor?

The answer to this question is quite obvious. For me to develop a sense of humor this late in the series would require a miracle, according to the ladies. Even my responses to each of the ladies were in my opinion slightly humorous. Marty and the rest of my poker pals felt the same as the ladies. According to Beth it was a no-win situation. She claims that I have her to take care of the humor part of the book. Cynthia thought that I had a slight chance on developing a sense of humor. She stated that if I wanted her to proclaim to the rest of the ladies that

I had a sense of humor that I would have to do something on the men's next poker night. My first response to her was that I had no clue as to what I needed to do since my previous attempts at obtaining a sense of humor failed. If you remember, I had a bad addiction to dog biscuits after I listened to a "No Sense of Humor" CD that I had purchased at the pet store. Cynthia then told me that if I shaved my head bald, wore a brown robe with sandals and sat on the floor with my legs crossed then and only then would she tell the ladies that I have a sense of humor. I could only imagine what would happen to the photos the men would take. When Harry Sr. read this portion of the survey, he said to me *"I give great haircuts."* while gently stroking his own baldness.

What is your favorite novelty used in the series?

My favorite novelty if you don't know by now is the flame-thrower. According to the ladies' responses, they each selected a different novelty as their favorite. I can tell you this. The least favorite novelty they chose was the "Man in the Box". Harriett made it a point to mention that item in her e-mail when she capitalized the words and underlined them along with the suggestion *"If you decide to use the Man in the Box on me I will make sure that your private parts are more than just a snack for Pixy and Dixy."* When I read Harriett's e-mail, the only word that came to mind was *"Ouch."* Harry asked me if I plan on using the "Man in the Box" in the next book. I told him *"No comment."* He then replied with a pun *"Dude, you really like playing with fire."*

Cindy also liked the use of the flame-thrower. After she enjoyed its use on the men, Cindy purchased a replica of the flame-thrower for her personal use. She even made a sad attempt to tell Marty that she felt safer with the flame-thrower whenever he was out of town. Brenda picked the His and Hers remotes. She was saddened to learn that this particular novelty was going to be phased out of the series. Bertha thought the use of the fake-beehives was extremely creative as it could be used in any story and was a kind of novelty similar to the flame-thrower that could adapt to any situation. Cynthia at first told me that she thought the use of the novelties were childish. She got that impression from Rick. Of course Cynthia sent me her response after she obtained the new "No sense of Humor" catalog from Cindy and placed her first order. Annie thought that the use of mechanical canines was very creative. In fact, she told the ladies that if she ever gets the chance to host one of the ladies special nights that she would place mechanical canines around her house to protect the ladies from would-be intruders, mainly the men. Harriett was particularly fond of the bubble gum that was in the form of condoms. She hoped that I plan on bringing that novelty back so she can use it to her advantage. In other words, be able to pull a revenge prank on Rick. Beth chose the bats. According to her, it allows the ladies to keep the men in line.

Who would you select to play the real therapist in the story "Therapy at Its Best"?

If it's true that people say history has a habit of repeating itself then the most logical choice would have been Marge. After all, she has come through in the past when the rest of the characters least expect it. In this case, the men were wise to the story-line and expected the therapist to be Marge, or at least Marty had hoped it would be her. Cindy tried to hire Marge but her old friend had a prior engagement. At one point Bertha was even considered for the role. Considering her stature in the series, the men wouldn't dare pull another prank on her. Marty learned that lesson the hard way when he surprised Bertha while wearing a Gorilla costume at her birthday party. Brenda and Annie tried to solicit the services of Jackie but she was also unavailable to play the part. Beth wanted to hire Mindy but the cost of a make-over was too great and it was not in our budget. So, who did the ladies choose? They chose Cynthia. She was the only character that came closest to resembling the photo on the therapist's business card. Actually, it was a photo of Cynthia but it was a photo that had been taken of her during her college years. Besides, she wanted the role so that she could use any personal information she got on Rick and post it to his dating profiles.

Who is your favorite pet character and why?

This question was by far the hardest for the ladies to answer. Many of the pet characters at one point would be considered a favorite based on the type of story that they were used in. My favorite has always been Ralph. In fact, a lot of people had told me that they liked the way I portrayed him. Many felt that they could relate Ralph's character with their own pets. Cindy was torn between Ralph and Tom. Ralph had first been a faithful pet when he was a pup, despite his sassiness and attitude towards Elizabeth's pets. She liked Tom because I transferred him from the leader of the Cat Mafia to Ralph's devoted partner. Harriett picked the "Yapper". Her old pet may have had it in for Daisy Mae and cost her and Harry a ton of money to buy him, but Mr. High Pockets was a canine who came through for his friends, no matter what the consequences were. Bertha also liked Mr. High Pockets. She found his character to be amusing. It always made her smile whenever she would read a story about his hijinks and how he ended up getting out of trouble, just like Ralph.

Annie liked Tom and Penny. She enjoyed the stories about how two cats could overcome diversity and be a welcomed addition in the canine world. Cynthia liked all of the pet characters. She stated that she would like them more if they did not have speaking roles. According to her, it would make people think that she is part of the group that is in dire need of a therapist. Brenda took a fancy to Max considering he was the only pet character with an education. I am sure somewhere down the line he will put his degree to good use and not just use it to build hot-tubs. Beth, considering she is the writing assistant, liked all of the pets. She plans on bring back several pet characters just to give Cindy that added edge for possible pranks.

Should the slate be wiped clean of all pranks between the men and the ladies?

As far as all of the ladies were concerned, they agreed with my ideas on keeping the tradition alive regarding the pranks among the adult characters. The ladies wanted to continue with the tradition of being superior over the men. Brenda was quoted as saying *"To let the men off the hook would be the same as letting them judge another beauty contest."* Believe it or not, the men felt the same way. After he read Brenda's comment *"Game on."*, Marty said *"She is so right."* and jotted down a few ideas on what he considered to be "Ultimate Pranks" that he wants to see take place in the next book.

Will Cindy actually write a book called "Book of Morons"? If so, who will be her publisher?

All of the ladies except Brenda thought that Cindy was joking when it was mentioned during one of their fun nights. The reason why Brenda knew Cindy was serious was because Cindy approached Brenda with the idea about the book before their title-quest began. In fact, Cindy wants Brenda to be her consultant. The book of course would be called the "Book of Morons". Just like everything else that we have started in the form of a tradition, Cindy's book would be similar to the "No Sense of Humor" series but with a few modifications. The "Morons" as Cindy would call them would be portrayed by the male characters, nothing knew there. But in her version, a lot of the names of different places and events would change. Let me give you a few examples. First, Cindy would change our Friday night poker events to "The Moron Club". Next, Ralph's entire novelty store and business would have a make-over. Cindy would change the name of the store to "Store for Morons" and on top of the store for publicity purposes would be a group photo of the men. Even the welcome mat would read *"Welcome to the Store of Morons."*

Ralph's Internet sales as well as the drive-thru would not change except for the type of novelties sold, mainly the t-shirts. I could only imagine what Bruce would be thinking when taking such orders. The customer would say *"I would like to order three medium Morons, two small*

Morons and two extra-large Morons. Oh, can I have the Morons gift wrapped please?" Another change Cindy would make would be the name of the city the canines currently live in. Instead of Dogville, the name would be changed to Moronville. Cindy would also change the names of the novelties by simply adding the word "Moron". Now imagine this for a moment. The fake-beehive would be called the "Moron Beehive". Instead of filling the novelty with candy, Cindy would replace the candy with photos of the male characters. It would be unique to hear someone say *"It's raining Morons."* as they stood underneath the beehive once it was opened.

Since we are on the subject of Morons, Cindy would bring back one novelty called His and Hers remote controls. She would have a special button added called the "Moron" button. On a trial run one day, Cindy gave a set to Eve to see if it would work. Eve told her that when she pressed the "Moron" button and pointed the remote at Harry Sr. that the remote didn't work. When asked why, Eve replied *"He is already a Moron."* Cindy also thought it would be a good idea to change the name of the famous flame-thrower. When used through the use of a modified selector-switch, everything that the weapon fired at would instantly turn into a Moron. If it were up to Mr. High Pockets, he would name it "The Moronator" and added *"Yeah, just add water."* Since Ralph was my publisher, Cindy chose Eli and Walter as her publishers.

SOPHIE WINS THE LOTTERY: THE CONCLUSION

Just as I walked into my apartment, Beth sent me a text message. She told me that she finally had a day selected where the ladies would all be together. I said to myself *"Finally."* Only one more story and I can relax and enjoy some time away from the office. For the time being, I found my time to be enjoyable when I read a note from Sophie. It said *"Out shopping. Be home later. Don't wait up."* I figured Sophie would be out shopping since she had won the Lottery. So I took advantage of the quiet time I had. Instead of my usual ritual of reading the newspaper, I decided to relax in my recliner and watch a movie. Wouldn't you know it that as soon as I got comfortable I received a text message from Samantha. It said *"Urgent. Meet me at the store."* I called Samantha to find out what was so urgent but all I got was a busy signal. Once again the thought *"What has Ralph done now?"* crossed my mind as I headed to the store.

There were two FBI vans parked in front of the store with their lights on when I arrived at the store. The front door was open and I saw several FBI agents take items from the store and put them in the vans. Samantha was in the lobby giving orders to other agents when I walked in the door. She said to me *"I am glad you are here."* I asked Samantha what was going on even though I had a sneaky suspicion that it had something to do with Ralph's latest plan on making canine currency. When she filled me in on the events, I looked at Samantha and said *"There is no way Ralph would do that."* Samantha agreed with me but because of the evidence that was against the canines along with the pressure her Director was getting, she had no choice but to arrest the canines. As we were discussing the plight of the canines, Samantha ordered another agent to confiscate Tom's lap-top as well as Beth's computer. I asked Samantha *"You don't think Beth is involved in this do you?"* Samantha shrugged her shoulders as she told me that anything was possible.

My go-to cat as she was commonly referred to then showed me the ledger Bruce had used to keep track of the donations. I said to Samantha *"I know. Ralph wanted to keep tabs on the donations for the Director of Camp Paws."* Samantha gave me a startled look and said *"You mean to tell me that you knew what Ralph was up to?"* I told Samantha that not only did I know about Ralph's plan but I also saw the printing plates he planned on using. She then said

"That's not good." Samantha quickly explained to me that if the prosecutor found out that I had any knowledge about Ralph's plan then he would use it to his advantage; mainly to prosecute the canines. With any luck, the prosecutor will not find out. I then told Samantha that I wanted to visit the canines to see how they were handling life behind bars for the time being. Samantha locked up the store and placed police tape around the yard. I then followed Samantha to the jail-house and hoped that before I arrived I would figure out a plan to get my canines out of jail.

Based on what Samantha had told me regarding the evidence and ironically put it *"Up a creek without a paddle.",* I called Beth to meet me at the jail-house. She may not have been a licensed attorney but she did possess a degree in criminology. I figured that Beth was the one adult character that could look out for the welfare of the canines and see to it that they get a fair trial.

Canine jail was not what Ralph and company had envisioned as a place that they would spend the rest of their lives in. It least it was better than an adult jail. Actually, canine jail was very similar to that of a plush animal shelter for canines. Which is why I could not understand how certain canines could complain about their treatment. To them, it did mean the loss of their freedom. As for our canines, losing their freedom meant that they lost their very existence. They no longer had the luxury to pull pranks. Despite having wall-to-wall carpeting, yard time, chew toys and three meals a day, our canines complained as if their lives were over. I think that if Ralph and company find a way to get out of their current situation that I will use that type of punishment the next time they get in trouble. Sophie would be furious if she could no longer have a Facebook page. Mr. High Pockets would no longer have the famous flame-thrower at his disposal. As far as Pixy and Dixy were concerned, being in canine jail would force the mighty warriors to go on a diet because of their over-indulgence with donuts. Their only problem later on would be for them to deal with those dreaded withdrawal symptoms.

As soon as Beth and I approached the cells, Ralph shouted *"Hey boss, we are glad you are here. Is it time to go?"* Beth asked the canines how could they let themselves be duped into such a scam. Everyone pointed at Ralph and said *"It was his idea."* Once our beloved canines made a plea for their release, I told them that I will see to it that they get released and then added *"Don't I always?"* I then grabbed Beth by the arm and told her we had a lot of work to do in changing the script. As we were about to leave the canine jail, Samantha stopped us and said *"I don't think you can save them this time."* I told Samantha I could and that it would just take a few moments for Beth and I to change the script. Samantha said *"Not this time."* and handed me a copy of the "No Sense of Humor" contract Ralph and I had signed. In the beginning, I prepared a contract for Ralph allowing me to bail him out through the use of script changes every time he got in trouble. However, there was an exception clause in the contract that stated for certain pranks or crimes, I was not allowed to make a script change. This was one of those exceptions. Samantha then said *"The canines have to fend for themselves."*

Discouraged was not the only feeling Beth and I felt as we left the jail-house. Beth certainly had her work cut out for her. The canine's fate rested in her hands. I felt bad to put Beth in that kind of stressful situation. Beth and I then went to the coffee chop to work out a strategy to save the canines. It didn't take long for Samantha to contact her with the court date for the canines. We were both shocked when we found out that the canine's day in court was scheduled for the next day. To make matters worse, Samantha's worst fear came true. A process server arrived at the coffee shop and handed me a subpoena signed by the prosecutor. It stated that I was to appear in court and testify on behalf of the State against the canines. I looked at Beth and said *"When it rains it pours."* and showed her the signature of the prosecutor. It was signed by Dog Thoroughbred III. We knew right then and there that the canines were in deep trouble considering Dog Thoroughbred worked for the Cat Mafia.

The Trial

When Marty and I arrived at the courthouse, we could see that the room was filled to capacity. The courthouse was filled entirely with felines. There were only a handful of canines present that sat behind the defense table to support Ralph and company. Beth had also arrived early.

I saw that she was busy laying out several folders on her table to prepare for the canine's defense. When the side door of the courtroom opened, many of the felines stood and hissed at Ralph and company as they entered the courtroom. Ralph looked at the felines, leaned to Beth and said *"Looks like our Gooses are cooked."* Tom, once again not understanding those phrases said to Ralph *"How come no one told me our Gooses are cooked? All I had to eat this morning was ham and eggs."* Pixy and Dixy attempted to return the favor to the crowd by giving their popular growl but all it did was anger the felines. Sophie was quiet and still angry. I noticed that she had worn one of her favorite outfits in an attempt to sway any of the jurors. Mr. High Pockets wore a business suit. We were lucky to see that he did not wear his popular camouflage outfit.

Before the crowd settled into their seats, the Bailiff escorted the Jury into the courthouse. As they took their seats, all eyes were on the canines. Tom said to Beth *"Oh crap."* as he pointed to several members of the Jury. Three of the members were former henchmen of the Cat Mafia. Tom kicked them out of the organization because they violated the code and turned against him. Suddenly, the courtroom erupted with cheers as Annie and Dog Thoroughbred made their entrance. Marty and I maneuvered our way through the crowd to sit behind the defense table. Marty attempted to lighten the mood and said to Beth *"Did you bring any Catnip?"* Beth looked at me and said *"Next time you want to sign a contract with Ralph, go through me first."* Before Beth could add another comment, the Bailiff called the court to order and announced the Judge. As luck would have it the Judge was a feline.

Once the court came to order, the Prosecutor made his opening remarks to the Jury. Dog Thoroughbred gave the Jury a description of the canines as if they were barbarians. He showed the Jury the evidence and said *"I will prove that those canines are guilty."* The spectators gave the Prosecutor a round of applause. Even the Jurors were grinning. When Beth gave her opening remarks, the felines shouted obscenities and even called her a traitor. She attempted to show the Jury the evidence she had in favor of the canines but the Jury would not have anything to do with it. They all looked the other way when she approached them. Disgusted, Beth returned to the defense table and said to us *"This is not going to be easy."* The Judge told the Prosecutor to present his first witness. He called an elderly feline to the stand. Through a series of questions, Dog Thoroughbred led the court to believe that the elderly feline was a victim of the counterfeit scam. He even showed the Jury photos of how the feline became impoverished. Beth objected to the witness testimony because the witness was not originally listed on the list. Of course the Judge said *"Overruled."* He told Beth to sit down and for the Prosecutor to present his next witness.

Dog Thoroughbred announced *"I call the Author to the witness stand."* I said to myself *"Oh boy, here we go."* I approached the witness stand hesitant to give my testimony. The Jury smiled when I took the stand.

Some even gave me a wink as if they knew what kind of testimony I was going to give. I could only imagine what the canines were thinking when Dog Thoroughbred approached me and began his examination. His first question to me was *"Did you have any knowledge of the canine's plan to produce money?"* I told the court I did know about Ralph's plan and as I was trying to explain to the court that Ralph did not know about the phony plates, the Prosecutor objected and asked the Judge to have my comment stricken from the record. The Judge agreed and when Beth objected, the Judge once again told Beth to sit down or he would find her in contempt of court. Dog Thoroughbred smiled as he knew he was getting his way. He then approached me with the evidence he had against the canines.

I gave the Prosecutor an evil look when he handed me the ledger. He asked me if I had seen the ledger. I told him yes and that the canines were using it as a record for the Director of Camp Paws. Dog Thoroughbred showed the ledger to the Jury and had them pay close attention to the pages that he marked. Inside the ledger were two pages of names and numbers in code that he portrayed to the Jury as a record of payments. Once again I tried to explain to the court that the ledger had been falsified but my comment was stricken from the record. After Annie whispered several comments to Dog Thoroughbred, the Prosecutor placed the rest of the evidence on a cart and wheeled it in front of the witness stand. One by one Dog Thoroughbred went over each item with the Jury.

He displayed the phony plates that the canines allegedly used, Tom's lap-top and the bags of the phony cash that were found in Sophie's possession. Several photos also had been shown to the Jury. Before the Prosecutor asked me questions regarding the items on the table, he noticed that several members of the Jury were yawning. He asked the Judge for a recess and the Judge ordered a one-hour cat-nap.

During the recess, Beth and I were discussing the possible fate of the canines when Samantha arrived. She asked us how the case looked for the canines and Beth responded *"Thanks to the Author's testimony, the canine's goose is cooked."* Suddenly, Pixy and Dixy were whispering to each other and soon it escalated into an argument. I asked Pixy what they were arguing about. He hesitated at first but Pixy turned to Ralph and said *"By the way, in case we don't make it, thanks for the donuts."* Ralph looked at Pixy and said *"What donuts?"* Pixy of course reminded Ralph of the donuts he sent to the house one day when the pair were printing up the canine money. Ralph then commented *"Are you sure. Because I didn't send you guys any donuts."* Beth asked Pixy why he waited until the trial to mention the receipt of the donuts. Pixy told us that they fell asleep afterwards and didn't want to get fired for sleeping on the job. I looked at Samantha and gave her a startled look. Pixy and Dixy may have their canine mishaps but they were two canines who had strong work ethics and would never fall asleep on the job intentionally.

I looked at Samantha and said *"Are you thinking what I'm thinking?"* Samantha smiled as our hunch led us to believe that Pixy and Dixy were drugged by the Cat Mafia. Even if that was true, it might not be enough evidence on the canine's behalf to set them free. At this point, the canines needed more than that to get them out of trouble. Samantha mentioned that the rest of the crime scene evidence had not been processed yet. Beth told Samantha to check out the crime scene and see if she could come up with any evidence that would help the canines. I told Samantha that time was not on our side and then added *"I go back on the stand in less than an hour."* Samantha left hoping to find anything that would save the lives of our precious canines. The clerk motioned for us to return to the courtroom. As we went back into the courtroom, Pixy whispered to his partner *"I should have known those donuts weren't from Ralph. He is such a cheapskate."*

The court came to order and I was once again asked to take the stand. Dog Thoroughbred stood in front of me smiling. When he wheeled the evidence cart closer to me he shouted out *"By the way Mr. Author, thank you for your testimony. You have been very helpful."* After he gave a brief wink at Annie, the prosecutor set his eyes on the evidence. Beth immediately stood as if she was going to object to the prosecutor's comment but stopped herself. She realized that the Judge would have held her in contempt of court so she sat down. When Dog Thoroughbred finished his series of questions, the felines in attendance once again applauded the prosecutor for a job well done. The Prosecutor gave Annie a high-five and then said to Beth *"He is all yours."*

Beth approached the witness stand with several photos in her hand. She handed me the photo of Ralph and Mr. High Pockets holding the canine plates in their paws. When she asked me if I recognized the photo, Dog Thoroughbred crossed his paws and shouted *"Objection."* Without hesitation, the Judge sustained the objection. This line of questioning continued as Beth attempted to show me several more photos. Each time the Prosecutor objected and the Judge yawned while he rendered his decision against Beth. Beth was so frustrated that she threw her arms in the air and returned to her seat. As she sat down, she mumbled to herself *"What a circus this is."* The Judge overheard Beth's comment and fined her for contempt of court. The Judge then excused me from the stand and asked the Prosecutor to present his next witness. Dog Thoroughbred smiled at the Jury, winked at Annie and then told the Judge *"The Prosecution rests."* Now it was Beth's turn. Still shaking from being held in contempt of court, Beth slowly took a drink of water as she pondered how to present her case. She realized that no matter what canine she would put on the stand that it would go against her. Her only way to save the canines rested with the hope that Samantha would come through for her. Beth then told the Judge *"The Defense rests."* After each side gave their closing arguments, the Judge sent the Jury to another room to render their verdict.

Meanwhile, Samantha was at Ralph's house with two other agents. They overturned everything they could find in an attempt to come up with any clue or evidence that would place the Cat Mafia at the scene. One of the agents dug through the trash and commented *"At least these canines know how to eat."* He showed the other agent that he found an empty box of donuts with a partially-eaten jelly donut inside the box. Samantha grabbed the box from the agent and told him to continue looking for more evidence. They were in luck. Lying on the floor on the other side of the printing press was a crushed jelly donut with a paw print. The print was of a cat. The agents gathered the evidence and headed to the FBI lab.

Samantha began the task of analyzing the donuts. She found that there were traces of sleeping pills inside the donut found in the box. After she ran the paw print through her database, Samantha got a hit. The computer showed that the print belonged to a Cat Mafia henchmen. On a hunch, Samantha checked the surveillance tapes in front of Ralph's house. All the tapes could show was a delivery person approach the house but she was unable to make out the appearance of the delivery person. She then sent two agents to the donut shop where the donuts had been purchased to review their cameras to see who bought the treats. The agents found that two felines bought the donuts the same time Pixy and Dixy had been drugged. They sent the footage to Samantha to see if she could identify the cats. The photo her agents sent her matched the photos in her data base. Samantha then sent the photos to Beth on her cell-phone and instructed her to have Tom look at the photos to see if he knew who they were. Tom looked at the photos and said *"Yeah, I know those guys. I kicked them out of the Cat Mafia when I was in charge. In fact, they are on the Jury."* Beth sent Tom's response to Samantha. The FBI agent told Beth to stall as much as possible as she would get to the courthouse with the evidence she had uncovered. Samantha place a call to one of the adult characters, grabbed the evidence and headed to the courthouse. She hoped that she was not too late.

Beth told me of the evidence Samantha found at Ralph's house. Just as we were going to tell our beloved canines of the evidence, the clerk announced that the Jury had reached a verdict. I looked at my watch and was more than startled to see that it took only 10 minutes for the Jury to reach a decision. We went back to the courtroom to take our places. Once the Bailiff called the court to order, the Jury walked in the room. They took their seats and looked at the canines as if they were about to meet their doom. The Judge said to the leader of the Jury *"Have you reached a verdict?"* The lead Juror told the Judge that the Jury had reached a verdict. When the Judge said *"How say you?"* the lead Juror responded *"We find the canines................"*

"Stop the proceedings." Samantha shouted when she burst her way into the courtroom. She was holding a paper high in the air and told the Judge that she had an order to stop the proceedings as well as release the canines. The Judge stood up and angrily shouted *"On whose authority?"*

Suddenly, a familiar voice was heard in the back of the courtroom saying "*On my authority.*" It was the First Lady. Chaos ensued inside the courtroom and once the agents handcuffed the Judge and the two Cat Mafia henchmen, it seemed that the canines were once again saved by that proverbial bell. Samantha approached Dog Thoroughbred and said "*Where's Annie?*" Apparently Annie had slipped away during the chaos.

After Marty obtained an autograph from the First Lady, he asked her why she saved the canines considering the pranks that had previous been pulled at the White House. She told Marty that despite wanting to have Mr. High Pockets stuffed and have him placed on the East Lawn as an ornament, the "Yapper" actually did her a favor. The First Lady found out that George was a plant by the Cat Mafia and planned on taking over the White House. She said to Marty "*One good turn deserves another.*" I asked Marty to take the canine's home so that I could talk to Beth. After the courtroom was cleared, I asked Beth "*So, quite different from a stolen dog-mobile huh?*" Beth smiled at me and as we were leaving the courthouse she asked me "*You didn't violate the contract and change the script did you?*" I told Beth "*Of course not.*" and added "*You know I don't have a sense of humor.*" Inside the trash can next to the defense table was the original script. Gee, I wonder how that got there.

IT'S ABOUT TIME

According to Cindy, it's been a long time coming. A chance for the ladies to settle who was the best story-teller and prankster. One would think that the ladies had their fill in book three. Just like the pet characters, it seemed that one quest was not enough. All of the ladies thought that it was about time to show the men how creative and cunning they truly are. For Beth and I, we felt it was about time the ladies decided to pick a date when we could host the award ceremony. Once the ladies agreed on a date, I had to figure out a place that we could use to pay tribute to the victor. The park was definitely out and for obvious reasons. Everyone had their fill of the famous park. I told the ladies that hosting the event in the park would create too much of an opportunity to have the event sabotaged by Annie. So, we all decided to host the ceremony at Cindy's house on an evening in which the men had to fore-go their traditional night of fun.

Before we delve into the results of the title-quest let's talk about the pet characters for a bit. Eli and Walter found that starting a new company was not as easy as it looked. They observed the pranks and listened to the stories but couldn't figure out how to put it all together. In the upcoming book they will receive lots of help from Beth and Brenda. Snowball never did get a chance to tell a story. She had been extremely busy with her new business. It's a good thing that she was considering what had happened to Sophie and the rest of the canines. As far as Ben was concerned, he was still listed as one of the favorite pet characters. Bertha and Brenda requested that I bring him back for future stories. They liked his cunning and especially liked his ability to keep a secret. Pixy and Dixy performed to their usual expectations. Hard to imagine how two canines that are proficient in firearms can be so gullible. And of course there is our beloved "Yapper". What can one say about Mr. High Pockets? He is definitely a character within a character, always trying to be the center of attention.

I am sure that most of you are wondering why there are not too many pranks played on Penny and Mary Ann. The answer is right in front of your nose. Think about this for a moment. Cindy controls her household. Harriett always gets her way with Harry. Eve can keep Harry Sr. from becoming a total slob just by cooking the right food. Even Beth to some degree can control my urges to pull a prank on my fellow comrades. So what does this tell you? It tells you that like the female adults characters, the female canines are in charge of their relationships. That is also true about Zeke even though he won't admit to the canines that his wife controls their household. Tom always tries to portray himself as the tough former Cat Mafia leader. After he had gone straight and became business partners with Ralph, his eloquent style of toughness went down the drain when he married Penny. Sophie is a canine who thinks that she should get her way no matter what. I told my beloved pet that even though she is considered the Author's favorite pet that she still had to earn her keep. Sophie coined the phrase *"It's about time."* when she won the Lottery. I am sure that thought would stick in her head if I gave her what she really wanted. My beloved pet wants to buy a house and become Ralph's new neighbor.

As usual, the round table was set up for the ceremony. It didn't take long for the round table to be considered a part of the tradition that the men had created. In preparation for the event, Cindy decorated the living room with banners and flowers. She even hired Pixy and Dixy to be her watch-dogs for the event. Not sure if she hired the canines to protect the ladies from Annie or if she hired them to protect the ladies from the men. Either way, Pixy and Dixy were given orders to attack when needed and ask questions later. Marty said to himself *"I can't wait until Rick arrives."* Cindy had already been informed that there was a possibility that Rick was going to bring a date to the ceremony. I wonder if it was Mindy. Instead of catering the event, all the ladies decided to bring food. The men were in charge of the alcohol except for Cindy's famous margaritas. Once again the stage was set. All we needed were the participants.

Eve and Harry Sr. arrived early to help Cindy with setting up the event. Harry Sr. only wanted to arrive early to get the best seat in the house so that he could demonstrate the effectiveness of his stretchy pants. Bertha also arrived early. She wanted to greet the men in a fashion that would best remember the event. Luckily for the men, Bertha left her latex gloves at home. When Cindy asked Bertha why she did not bring her gloves, Bertha responded *"Who needs gloves when we have Pixy and Dixy."* It must have been hard for Cindy to visualize Bertha's comment when she saw that Pixy and Dixy were sitting near the front door eating donuts. Brenda and Beth arrived together. Why not considering the pair have a lot in common. Of course Marty couldn't resist a comment when he saw Rick and Cynthia arrive together. He said *"I see you two love-birds made up."* Once Cynthia gave Marty an evil look she whispered something in Cindy's ear. Cindy smiled without revealing what Cynthia said to her but shouted *"I know what you mean. At least you get to leave afterwards."*

I arrived in the nick of time to keep Marty from getting into trouble. As soon as he saw me, Marty said *"It's about time."* and poured me a drink. Once I saw the look Cindy was giving her husband, I instantly knew why Marty was being so nice to me. He needed re-enforcements. That also came true when Harry and Harriett arrived. Knowing that the terrible foursome was present allowed Marty to believe that he was safe from the wrath of the ladies. When Anna arrived, I jokingly said to Marty *"Speaking of re-enforcements."* After Anna hugged the ladies, she told Cindy that she had a present for Marty. Marty gave Anna that ever-so-popular evil look when he opened the package and found that Cynthia gave him a bottle of hair tonic. Once the men stopped laughing, Anna said to Marty *"Maybe your hair will grow back in the next book."*

While we were waiting for Adam to arrive, I decided to have a little fun of my own. I noticed that the gift Cindy received from Zeke was displayed on a corner table in the living room. I went up to Cindy and asked her *"Would you mind if I had a little fun?"* When I told her what I wanted to do, she grinned and said *"Go for it."* I refilled my drink and rejoined the men. A few minutes later, I shouted out to Cindy *"Hey Cindy. What's in the box?"* Cindy told the gang that it was gift from Zeke. Marty looked at his wife and said *"I didn't know he gave you a gift."* Cindy then told the gang the uniqueness of the sphere without revealing the truth. She told everyone that whenever someone holds the sphere that it glows. Marty's curiosity got the better of him as he said *"Oh yeah."* He picked up the sphere and was amazed at the colors that he saw. Marty then added *"This is neat."* As soon as Cindy gave me a wink, I sprang into action. I said to Marty *"Hey Marty. How does your wife look in a tie?"*

Previously, when Marty told us of the real story of what had happened that evening, he told the guys that his wife had put on a few extra pounds but knew better to say anything about it to his wife. Instead, Marty blurted out *"Oh, my wife looked awesome in that tie."* Cindy immediately crossed her arms when she saw that green mist emerge from the sphere. Both Cindy and I knew Marty was lying. Rick saw that Marty was having fun with the sphere and wanted in on the action. He rose from his seat and grabbed the sphere while saying *"Let me see that."* I tapped Harry on the arm and said *"Watch this."* Cynthia must have caught on to the prank as she looked at me and pointed her finger at me as if it was a gesture for me to keep quiet. I then shouted to Rick *"Hey Rick. Have you and Cynthia been on another romantic date?"* Like before, as soon as Rick told the group no, a green mist once again created another aura of imperfection. Harry Sr. felt that he was being left out. He immediately buttoned his pants and held the globe close to his face. When he commented on the colors that vividly displayed itself inside the sphere, Harry shouted *"Hey Pop. Did you like Mom's cooking last night."*

According to Harry, he received a phone call earlier in the day from Harry Sr. as all he could do was complain about the meal Eve had cooked for him. Harry Sr. smiled at his wife and said *"That was the best meal ever."* Eve smiled at her husband and told the ladies that her cooking was the one trait her husband loved about her. Luckily for Harry Sr. his wife did not see the green mist come out of the sphere when he commented on Eve's cooking. Eve's smiled turned to an evil look when Anna whispered to Eve the real purpose of the sphere. After that look, I wanted to see to it that the ladies see their husbands in their true form. Pretending to refill my drink, I turned off the lights in the living room. I could tell that the ladies were amused when they saw their husband's faces glow in the dark like a neon sign in a red-light district. Before the men caught wind of the prank, I immediately turned the lights back on. It did not take long for the men to realize what had happened to them. I looked at my watch and wondered when Adam was going to arrive. This was one time that I needed re-enforcements.

Luck once again prevailed on my side when Adam finally arrived. Harry said to me *"It's amazing to see that you always get saved by the bell."* Adam walked over to the ladies and presented them with their much-needed victory bottle of Scotch. Marty tried to close the door but when a foot reached into the doorway blocking him from closing the door he said to himself *"Oh crap."* Standing at the door was Elizabeth. She looked at Marty and said *"What happened to you? You look like a neon bowling ball."* Before Marty could provide a come-back of his own, Cindy rushed to the door to greet her mother. Harry Sr. asked Marty *"Hey. What's old battle-ax doing here?"* Marty told the crafty veteran Cindy invited her. He then told the gang that he thinks his wife invited her mother to spite him. We all looked at each other and knew Marty was right.

While the ladies were busy gossiping, the men were staring at the ladies wondering when the ceremony was going to start. Harry Sr. was hungry even though he had already gouged himself on several plates of food. Marty was getting impatient also. It was hard for him to accept that he didn't get a chance to provide his mother-in-law with a jovial come-back. Cindy told the ladies that the ceremony would start after she went to get refills for their drinks. As soon as Cindy was out of sight, Marty said to himself *"Time to get even."* When no one was watching, Marty pulled out Zeke's old ray gun and zapped Elizabeth. He then quickly hid the ray gun and acted as if nothing had happened. For some reason, the topic of the ladies conversation turned to Elizabeth when she was asked a question by Beth. Elizabeth attempted to clear her throat and found that she was not able to answer Beth's question.

Cindy noticed the commotion around the table when she returned with a tray of margaritas. She asked Beth what was wrong when she noticed that the ladies were huddled around her mother. Beth said to Cindy *"I'm not sure. I think your mother might have laryngitis."* Cindy placed the tray on the table and asked her mother what was wrong. Elizabeth made the attempt to talk but found that her lips were moving and couldn't hear the words. Cindy then turned to look at the men and saw Marty snickering while looking away from the ladies. She also saw the rest of the men snicker and realized what her husband had done. Cindy looked at her husband and said *"You are such a Moron. Now fix it."* When Marty saw Cindy grab the "Marty" bat, he went to the chair that Harry Sr. was sitting in to retrieve the ray gun. Marty hid the ray gun under the seat while Harry Sr. was in the bathroom. Suddenly, Harry Sr. left the food table and returned to his seat. Just as he was about to sit down, Marty shouted *"Wait. Don't sit down."* Unfortunately for Marty, Harry Sr. was not quick enough to react to Marty's request. Everyone heard a crunching sound when Harry Sr. sat down. Harry Sr. said *"What the......."* He placed the plate of food on the end table and reached under the cushion. Marty was shocked when he saw that Harry Sr. was holding the ray gun now in several pieces. To add to Marty's dilemma, Harry Sr. tossed the ray gun at Marty and said *"Next time tell your kids to put away their toys."*

The phrase "Saved by the Bell" has been used in several stories to show how lucky the men were. This was another time I had to save Marty. I saw that Cindy was about to use the Marty bat on her beloved husband and quickly ran up to Cindy. I told our host that the effects of the ray gun will wear off shortly. Before any more pranks could be performed, I asked Beth if she could start the ceremony. Beth gathered the ladies around the table and toasted the ladies for their efforts. Adam also toasted the ladies with the bottle of Scotch he had brought. He said to the ladies *"To the victor."* Luckily for the men, they were included in the toast. After all, it was a family tradition.

Beth resumed her role as the host of the contest. She grabbed the envelope from her purse and announced *"And the winner for best female story-teller and prankster goes to..........all the ladies."* Cindy and the rest of the ladies looked at each other wondering why no specific lady had been selected. Beth told the gang that since it was the last title-quest that the Judges decided to honor all of the ladies. She told the ladies that she felt it was more important to keep the friendships alive and well rather than create more competition between the ladies. Beth raised her glass in the air, smiled and then said to the ladies *"Besides, we have to spend our time keeping the men in line."* The men whole-heartedly agreed with Beth. Soon, everyone was seen enjoying the spoils of victory. It was nice to see that once again the ladies forgave the men. I was proud in knowing that I was part of that family tradition. I said to myself *"It's about time."*

Like all things in life, there are some occasions that end as swiftly as they had started. At least I was ready to continue the tradition that kept the series alive and well. As I was getting ready to leave Cindy's house, I mentioned to Marty *"Don't worry about the hair tonic. You won't be needing it."* Harry gave me a startled look as we walked out the door and said to me *"Why won't Marty be needing that hair tonic?"* I placed my arm on Harry's should and said *"I plan on keeping him bald in the next book."* I knew Harry wanted to smile but he caught himself when he said to me *"I would have normally smiled at that comment you made."* and then added *"If you had a sense of humor."*

ABOUT THE AUTHOR

Unlike in previous books where Author's write about themselves in the third person on the back cover of the book, I decided to change that approach. Not only am I going to give you a mini-autobiography but give you answers on several questions that many of my readers have asked me in the past.

Originally, I was born and raised in a small town called Methuen, Massachusetts. It borders New Hampshire, the place where I grew up and lived for almost 18 years. I come from a family that has its roots deep in French-Canadian ancestry. I am the oldest of three brothers and proud of the fact that on my Father's side, there are only men and have been for over six generations. Now you can see why I write about traditions in the books. My childhood was neither boring nor tremendous. One could say it was routine except for the fact that since my family is Catholic, I went to Parochial school until I went to High School. During my final year in High School, I joined the Army under the Delayed-Entry program. A few months later I attended

Basic training at Ft. Leonard Wood, Mo. Soon thereafter I found myself serving the first of many tours in Germany.

My military career spanned a total of 18 years, 16 of which was spent on active duty along with 2 years in the reserves. Nine of my 18 years was spent in Germany on three different tours. I even spent two summers at West Point training 3rd year Cadets as well as a couple of state-side tours in between. Probably the best time I had in the military was during my last tour at Ft. Leonard Wood, Mo. when I returned to become a Drill Instructor. I wanted to stay an additional year as a D.I. but the Army was downsizing at the time and would not approve the additional year. To top off my military career, I rejoined the Army 10 years later to join a reserve outfit in Wisconsin as a reserve D.I.

During that great career, my children were born. My son Nicholas was born in Germany at the Nuremburg Army Hospital and my daughter Brittany was born in Fitchburg, Massachusetts. Brittany was the first female born on my Father's side of the family. She was the one who broke the tradition. If there ever was time that I wanted to break the tradition, it was when Brittany was born. What a blessing. After my first divorce and during my last tour of duty in Frankfurt, Germany my other daughter Stephanie was born. She was less than two months old when I had received orders to attend the Drill Sergeant Academy at Ft. Leonard Wood, Mo. About three days prior to graduation, I received a notice from Red Cross that my daughter Stephanie passed away. Luckily for me that my unit commander and I served together in Germany and he allowed me to take permissive TDY to take care of my family matters and return to graduate with the class. My other two children currently live in Massachusetts near my two brothers.

About four years after I left active duty, I decided to further my education and used my old G.I. Bill to put myself through College. I attended night courses at the Truman Education Center on Ft. Leonard Wood, Mo. where I attained two separate Associate Degrees from Central Texas College, one in Business Management and one in Business Administration. I finally achieved my Bachelor's Degree in Criminal Justice from Columbia College in 2013. Yes, I do have plans to pursue my Master's degree once book nine is published.

Now it's time to answer that proverbial 64,000 dollar question. Many friends and readers have asked me what gave me the idea to write a book and why. Another frequently asked question was where I get my ideas from.

To start, there were several contributing factors that led me to write the first book. Sophie was the main factor. I adopted Sophie in March of 2011 and it was by chance we ended up together. I originally adopted another dog but on the day I went to the animal shelter to pick her up, the Director of the shelter contacted me and said that the dog was no longer available for adoption because the dog had Parvo. Since I was already on my way to the shelter, I decided to look for another dog. When I saw Sophie I thought she was cute so the attendant at the shelter told me to fill out the paperwork in another room and spend time with Sophie while I was doing it. The entire time I filled out the paperwork Sophie had placed her head on my lap. Of course I knew then that she was the one.

About five days after I had taken her home, Sophie became ill. She was so ill that the Vet told me that there was a good chance she would not survive the illness. Sophie came down with three viruses; a distemper, influenza and a micro-plasma virus. It got to a point that my three month old dog had a 105 degree fever and had not eaten in 8 days. Sophie's weight had dropped to 22 pounds. The Vet did all he could to keep her on an IV and give her antibiotics to reduce the fever. He gave me a prescription card so that I could purchase medicated dog food. For the next four days, I hand-fed Sophie until she was able to eat on her own. Everyone was truly amazed at Sophie's recovery. In fact, Sophie's recovery photo was posted on the back cover of book one.

Sophie's antics for the next few months led me to believe that she definitely possessed a sense of humor. One day while I was working on a homework assignment on my lap-top, Sophie nudged my arm with her nose and immediately started a series of antics around the house. I said to myself *"Sophie, I should write a book about you."* That was the turning point which gave me the idea to write the series. As luck would have it, I had just finished my finals in a Criminal Law class and found that I had a lot of downtime before the next class started. After doing some much needed research on various kinds of humor regarding people and their pets, book one went public the day after Christmas in 2012. Book one started out as a project book since I wanted to see if I had the ability to change my writing skills after spending numerous hours writing academic papers for College. The rest is history.

Now, you are probably wondering about the stories. All of the stories I have written are purely fictional. The adult characters are also fictional with the exception of one; the writing assistant. She is an actual person who works at a local bank in my area. All of the pet characters are fictional except Sophie and the pets I had mentioned in books one and two. Snowball and Mya were former pets. Mya was given away to a little girl who had lost her pet. Snowball was given to a family because I could not keep two pets. The only other item that is real is the copy of the post card that I had received from the President of the United States.

THE WHITE HOUSE
WASHINGTON

I would like to extend my deepest thanks for your kind gift. Your generosity is much appreciated.

I am humbled by the thoughtfulness of the American people and honored to serve as President. If we join together in common purpose, I am confident that we will solve the great challenges of our time.

Thank you, again, and I wish you all the best.

Sincerely,

The Presidential Post Card

Back in July of 2013, I sent the President a copy of my first three books as a kind gesture. Two months later I received a post card from the President thanking me for the kind gift. Even though I don't have a sense of humor, I sent the President an e-mail thanking him for the response. I also told the President that if he wanted me to autograph the books to be sure to include an invitation to the White House in his next response. Yes, I am still waiting for that e-mail. To this day, I still have the post card and the original envelope it came in. It was a welcome addition to my "No Sense of Humor" wall.

The Author

"If I end up getting a sense of humor, I will shave my head bald, buy a brown robe and become a Tibetan Monk. At least they have Wi-Fi."

Dedicated to the ladies at my local bank for
their contributions to the story-line.

*"If I would have known that I would have been treated
this good when I opened my bank account, I would have
done it months ago. Sure beats getting a toaster."*